THE DYING MAN'S CLUES

Derek Heater

Pen Press Publishers Ltd

First published in Great Britain by
Pen Press Publishers Ltd
39, Chesham Road
Brighton
BN2 1NB

ISBN 1-905621-23-X

Printed and bound in the UK

A catalogue record of this book is available from
the British Library

Cover design by Jacqueline Abromeit

Dramatis Personae

It should be noted that many of the characters referred to, or appearing, in this story, are historical persons. Those marked * are in this category; those marked † are unnamed but are persons holding the specified positions at the time.

Residents of Brighthelmston with official positions
*Rev John Dring, curate of St Nicholas Church
*Rev Thomas Hudson, vicar of St Nicholas Church
†Sexton, St Nicholas Church
*William Wade, Master of the Ceremonies
*Mr Wigney, High Constable, parish of Brighthelmston and West Blatchington

Shopkeepers and other residents of Brighthelmston
Pierre-Auguste, Chevalier de St Paul, French *émigré*
*Edward Cobby, undertaker, shopkeeper and author
*John Dine, shoemaker
*James Gregory, owner of circulating library
*Martha Gunn, 'queen' of the dippers
*Susan Haymes, dressmaker
*Dr Richard Henderson, physician
Henry, manservant to Mr Hamilton
*Thomas Kemp, landowner

Louis Lefebvre, a.k.a. Lemaître, French secret agent
*'Smoaker' Miles, bather
Charlotte Patcham, wife of George Patcham
George Patcham, shopkeeper
Henrietta Patcham, daughter of George and Charlotte Patcham
Jane Patcham, niece of George and Charlotte Patcham, affianced to Jonathan Preston
James Preston, bookseller
Jonathan Preston, artist, son of James Preston
Mary Preston, daughter of James Preston
Mr Williams, gentleman's outfitter

Residents of Rottingdean
*Thomas Beard, landowner
Betsy, Rev Sydenham's horse
Billy, Rev Sydenham's cat
*John Dudenay, shepherd
Mrs Heath, widow and Rev Sydenham's landlady
*Rev Dr Thomas Hooker, vicar of St Margaret's Church
Rev Benjamin Sydenham, curate of St Margaret's Church
Will Watson, smuggler
†Officer in charge of Customs House

Residents of Hove
Ebenezer Elliott, villager
Dan, Mr Elliott's dog
Preston family (before start of story)

Persons in official national or local positions
†Adjutant, military camp
*Admiral Lord Bridport, naval commander
†Barrack Master, infantry barracks
†Commanding Officer, military camp
Dubois, British secret agent
*Henry Dundas, Secretary of State for War and Colonies
Fabre, British secret agent
*Lord Grenville, Foreign Secretary
*Gerald Hamilton, MP for Haslemere, owner of
Marlborough House
*Evan Nepean, Department of War and Colonies, key
figure in home and foreign secret services
Ned North, coastguard
*Rt Hon Thomas Pelham, MP for Sussex and Deputy
Lieutenant
*George, Prince of Wales
*Caroline, Princess of Wales
*Duke of Richmond, Lord-Lieutenant
Silas Smith, army private
*Commodore Borlase Warren, naval commander
*William Wickham, minister plenipotentiary in Berne,
Switzerland; formerly superintendent of aliens,
Home Office
Private Yates, soldier

Chapter 1

There was no doubt, in the stillness of that cold evening, that the sharp crack was a pistol shot. It certainly startled my elderly chestnut mare Betsy. But we soon pulled ourselves together, and I urged her, at the fastest trot she could manage, along the road in the direction from which the sound of the detonation had come – our way home, in any case.

Although the sky showed the dull tones of a gloomy, heavily clouded dusk, there was enough light filtering through the louring mass of dark grey cloud to see, after we had covered about a quarter of a mile, a stationary horse and its erstwhile rider prostrate on the ground. The dim illumination also enabled me to see another rider, forcing his horse on away from the static scene at a considerable gallop – a speed that no doubt conjured up in Betsy's mind remembrances of her own sprightly youth in melancholy contrast to the limitations of her old age. It was fairly obvious that this fleeing figure was the person who had fired the shot, and, hearing our relatively hurried approach, took off for fear of being recognised.

Having reached the victim, I dismounted. Any attempt to chase the gunman was quite out of the question; and besides, my first thought was to try to help this poor injured person. He was a youngish man, probably mid-twenties, of handsome appearance, tall, with jet-black hair and neatly dressed. He was quite evidently mortally wounded.

It was evident, too, that he desperately wanted to tell me something. His hand feebly caught the lapel of my coat in an

1

effort to draw me closer. His voice was faint, barely audible, and his speech faltering; he gasped painfully at the effort to produce the words. As near as I can transcribe his message, in the way I interpreted it in those few tense moments, this is what he said: 'mmm ... gun ... er ... private ... er ... meeting ... mmm ... h-hook ... er ... prints.' While concentrating to understand what he was telling me, I was cradling his head in my arm. I felt it subside as he passed away.

As I shall relate in a little while, I am an ordained priest. So, I blessed him to ease his soul's flight to Heaven.

The next task was to identify him. Yet this proved impossible. No money. No letters. No papers; except for a couple of etched pictures, scattered from an otherwise empty saddlebag lying beside the body. Perhaps the motive for the attack was theft, a theft virtually complete when Betsy and I disturbed the perpetrator? What was I to do? I had never before experienced violence, and I have never been terribly quick-witted at the best of times, so it was not surprising that the dilemma I then faced further slowed my attempt to make a decision.

But before retailing my thoughts and consequent actions, I owe it to you, dear reader, to explain who I am and to describe my whereabouts that evening.

My name is Benjamin Sydenham, graduate of Oxford University. Now, in the leisure of my retirement, with the aid of the detailed diary I kept at the time, and of my wife's superior memory to correct and add to mine, I am setting down this narrative. My purpose is to ensure that the little historical episode into which I was thrown as a minor actor, by the accident of my presence at the murder, shall be remembered in accurate, undistorted detail. Also, to be truthful, I am old enough now not to be unduly embarrassed by my stupidities in making so many mistakes in my self-appointed effort of tracking down the murderer. For, that is what I resolved to do and it was in pursuit of this purpose that led to my being involved in the tangled and dramatic events that unfolded.

The year was 1795; and the story I shall be narrating took place in late May to mid-June. I, like the murdered man as I guessed, had not yet reached 30 years of age (I was born in 1769), though I was decidedly less handsome than he: mousy haired and lanky of stature as I was. At that time I held the position of curate at St Margaret's Church in the Sussex coastal village of Rottingdean. I lodged in a cottage, looked after by the kindly elderly widow Mrs Heath, who owned it, following the death of her husband.

At that time the village had a population of some 500 souls, a substantial figure, yet far exceeded by the size of the flocks of sheep. That relatively large number of human inhabitants was sustained by a thriving economy based on its recent development as a resort for visitors in the summer season, its traditional activities of agriculture and fishing, and, to be honest (or dishonest!), the newly burgeoning smuggling. Access to the sea – the English Channel – was made possible by a natural breach in the soft chalk cliffs; hence the name given to the way down to the shingle beach, namely, the Gap. The whiteness of the cliffs indeed reveals the nature of the firm but porous foundations of the hills, called the Downs, which gently rise to the north of the coastline. The untilled stretches are covered with the mutton- and wool-producing grass. Sussex mutton was indeed famous. Mr James Gregory, who owned the circulating library in The Steyne (a part of the town of Brighthelmston) wrote at the time of my story that: 'It is supposed that there is no spot in the universe which produces finer mutton than that fed on these Downs. The exquisite flavour of the meat is owing to the lands being entirely free from marsh or swamp, the salubrity of the air, the fine quality of the grass, and the abundance of aromatic herbs with which it is intermingled.'

But, for the moment, enough of dull background, even though it is essential to my tale.

As I was trying to concentrate my mind, the thought occurred to me that it was only by chance that I had chosen to use the road running beside the coast rather than the inland bridle-way. If I had not, Betsy and I would not have startled the assailant. Such is the power of fortuitous choice and events in determining the history of nations, and the lives of even the most insignificant of individuals. I was by then beginning to focus on my task.

The dead man's distressed horse was facing towards Brighthelmston, which is some four miles to the west of our village. Therefore, it was reasonable to assume that he was making his homeward journey from, perhaps, Newhaven, the harbour town to the east, or even Rottingdean; though he was not resident in the village or I would have recognised him. I was myself returning from an evening visit to my friend, Thomas Hudson, vicar of St Nicholas Church the parish church of Brighthelmston (or 'Brighton', as some folk were then starting to call the town, in lazy abbreviation; I, conservatively, still prefer the full form). My thinking ran along these lines: since I was returning from a visit to a place where I was barely known, could not the murdered man have similarly been making a visit to Rottingdean, where he was barely known?

I decided, accordingly, to sling the body over his saddle, gather up the bag and scattered pictures and escort my mournful find into the village. After all, we were much nearer to Rottingdean than Brighthelmston; also I could take horse and man to the vicarage and seek the help of my vicar, the Rev Dr Thomas Hooker.

Hooker! When the dying man mumbled, 'mmm... h-hook... er', was he, in his last seconds, telling me that he knew Dr Hooker, that the vicar might be aware in some way of the purpose behind the killing? There was, in truth, a slightly shady side to that religious man's life. Do not misunderstand me. Thomas was a splendid fellow and we enjoyed a close bond of friendship beyond our formal clerical ties; he was only seven years older than me. He was a well-liked and respected figure in the village. In fact, when he died, only a year before I started to set down this account of the events of the summer of 1795, his

4

parishioners wrote in the Brighthelmston local newspaper:

How chang'd, alas! Is now dear Rottingdean!

Where not one smiling face is to be seen;

Ask you the reason? We reply anon,

Our kind and much lov'd pastor! He is gone!

Doggerel, but written with a heart-felt sincerity that brought a lump to my throat when I read it.

Was the murder, I wondered, connected with smuggling? There – the nature of Thomas Hooker's moonlighting – literally – is out! Several Rottingdean houses, including the vicarage, have cellars and connecting tunnels for storage of contraband goods. Surreptitiously, my vicar acted as a look-out man for the smugglers – to warn them in the event of the approach of officers marshalled to seize the illegally imported goods and their clandestine importers. This was a hazardous business because there is a customs house in the High Street between the vicarage and the Gap. However, Thomas believed that God would consider his association with this illegal trade a venial sin, perhaps even hardly that. The duties on tobacco and brandy were swingeing. And what man of the cloth can survive without these commodities! Especially when they were so easily transported from France – even though, since 1793, Britain had yet again been at war with her continental neighbour.

To return to the thread of my story. Raising the body on to the man's horse was a hugely difficult task. His, literally, dead weight and the agitated nervousness of his horse drained my modest muscular strength, and the effort consumed a considerable amount of time. At last, Betsy and I were able to lead our cortège slowly to the village. We turned left up the High Street and duly arrived at the vicarage, set to the east of the 'Waste', the common land and pond. It was damnably late by now, if the reader will forgive the profane word, but it reflects my agitated state of mind that evening. Yet it seemed imperative that I disturb Dr Hooker. In any case, in my heart, I knew that, considerate Christian as he was, he would express no anger. On the contrary, he would want to be fully involved:

to assist in identifying this, as yet unknown, man; to restore him to his loved ones, thus ensuring his interment in consecrated ground; and, if at all possible, to contribute to the apprehension and consequent punishment of his murderer.

On our slow, gingerly paced way to the vicarage I had another thought. The poor man's words were haunting me. Indeed, apart from the infernal bleating of the sheep – to which I had not become accustomed (or hardened!) – I had nothing else to occupy my mind. If I had solved the riddle of 'h-hook... er', what of his other words? 'Gun' surely referred to the weapon that killed him. And there could just as surely be no question that 'prints' referred to the etchings I had found. How many more had there been? Why did the victim have them in his saddlebag? Why was the assailant interested in them? And then, of course, what connection did they have with the murder? Finally, 'private ... er ... meeting'. How might it be possible to discover where and when that would take place?

When we reached the vicarage, a handsome building dating back half a century before the events I am retailing, and constructed on the glebeland between the church and the smithy, I lowered the body to the ground to relieve the horse of its weight. The wretched beast hung its head sadly, fully aware of the fate of its master. I knocked on the door, which was soon opened by Thomas; he was not yet abed, but reading.

'Hello, Ben,' he said. 'You still abroad at this late hour? Had a good gossip with my namesake of St Nicholas, did you?' He paused for a second, looking at me intently. 'I must say, you do look tired and worried. Anything the matter?'

In a few sentences I told him of the dead man lying outside, how I had come to bring him to the vicarage, including my belief that in his dying words he had mentioned the name 'Hooker'. The vicar rushed from the hallway and together we bore the body into the house, where we laid it on a sofa. Thomas looked carefully at the man, went outside again and quickly returned.

6

'No,' he admitted, 'I have no idea who this man is, nor why he should have given such priority in the last moments of his life to mentioning my name. What is more, I do not even recognise his horse.'

This was not a flippant comment. The reason for the remark was that Thomas himself was a skilled rider and inveterate hunter. Through such interest he knew every horse of his acquaintances as well as he knew their owners. He was also now looking very worried.

'We must think carefully,' he continued. 'We must work out the quickest way of identifying him so that we can return him to his family and, if the poor fellow lived in Brighthelmston, to assist the town's constable to apprehend the dastard who committed this atrocious deed.'

'Apart from what he tried to tell me, the prints are the only clue we have,' I said.

'Of course!' Thomas almost shouted. 'I've seen framed etchings like these in Mr Beard's house. Supposing this young man here was returning from selling some more to him? Go over there quickly and ask – never mind rousing him.'

I ran as swiftly as I could past the pond and, arriving at the house, knocked on the door of Thomas Beard's fine, sturdily built house (another Thomas – there are four in my narrative). He eventually opened up, looking mightily displeased to be visited so late. Nevertheless, my brief explanation turned his manner in an instant to profound concern, so we were soon hastening together back to the vicarage, though he, being used to agricultural work and of tougher build, yet two years my junior, was well ahead when we arrived.

Immediately our neighbour saw the dead man, he collapsed distraught into the nearest chair and buried his face in his hands. 'May God in His infinite mercy forgive me,' he cried.

Thomas Hooker and I stared at each other in perplexity. It was inconceivable that Mr Beard, a virtuous member of the community, a leading landowner from a family of many generations in the village, could have waylaid, robbed and killed the young man lying now in front of him.

Aided by comforting words from Dr Hooker, Mr Beard was eventually able to explain. 'That poor, wretched fellow is Jonathan Preston. His father owns a small shop in the narrow lanes of Brighthelmston, where he sells books, maps and prints.' He turned to the vicar, and asked, 'Thomas, you must surely have bought a volume or more from him?'

Dr Hooker sadly acknowledged that he had, but had never seen the son. That the two recovered prints must have come from that shop, he now realised.

Mr Beard went on: 'Jonathan has – oh, my word – had a studio in the attic, where he made the etchings and the prints from them. I had arranged that he should visit me late this afternoon with a selection of his newest. I was to buy a few and he was to advise me on the best places in the house to hang them. To my utter shame – and my conscience will suffer for the rest of my life – having spent the best part of the day in my fields, I went to 'The Black Horse' to slake my thirst. I fell to talking, and one pint led to another. Jonathan, dear fellow, waited for me in the house. Following my delayed return home, we completed my purchase, after many changes of mind on my part and the sharing of a pie between us. This is why he was riding back to Brighthelmston so much later than he had planned. And that is why I feel so responsible for his death.'

His voice cracked with emotion during his painfully remembered explanation. But he soon composed himself and stated in firm tones that would brook no contradiction what was to be done: 'It is imperative that we take Jonathan home with all speed. He was expected well before nightfall. His father – and his sister, Mary – will be beside themselves with worry. How awful that their worry is justified! I will now go to my nearest barn, collect a cart and return to put our dreadful load in it, with a clean rug on which to lay the body. Thomas,

8

you will stay here in case anyone saw your curate on the way here and comes to make enquiries. You, Ben, will come with me, leading Jonathan's horse and carrying a lantern, though, thanks be to God, the cloud is starting to break more and moonlight is clearly glinting through in places.'

He left, and reappeared shortly. Our journey was agonisingly slow, given the urgency of our mission. The farm-horse plodded, the cartwheels and axles creaked and groaned, while Jonathan's horse walked head-down in misery. The sweet-rank smell of rotting seaweed reached us from the beach below, where it had been thrown by the recent wind-forced waves. Neither Mr Beard nor I felt like talking, he left to his self-recrimination, I, to my tantalising puzzle of Jonathan's desperate message. Indeed, the mood of the journey triggered a haunting memory, hitherto suppressed, of Jonathan's pleading eyes, willing me to understand his barely coherent clues.

On arrival at the entrance to the maze of little lanes and alleys nearest to the Prestons' combined home, shop and studio, we halted. Mr Beard again took charge.

'I shall go to break the dire news to the family,' he said, 'while you stay here. When I come back with Mr Preston we shall take the body into his home, and the horse to a place where he directs us. I shall then accompany him back to his home and wait there while you go off to rouse Mr Wigney, the High Constable.'

He then gave me clear instructions where to find the constable's office-cum-residence and walked briskly away.

He returned in due course with an utterly broken Mr Preston. I noticed – a trivial and so utterly unsuitable an observation that I wondered why I had made it – that he sported a queue or pigtail, as it was sometimes called. I then remembered that his son did also, as did I at that time. It was a hairstyle that was no longer much in vogue, so I warmed to Mr Preston for his refusal to be dictated to by fickle fashion. While the father gazed tearfully at his son, Mr Beard explained that Mary

Preston was too overcome with grief to come out to look upon her brother. Mr Beard and I then carried Jonathan, though Mr Preston insisted on taking care of the horse – easier for him to do that than give instructions. As we carried our burden into the shop, Miss Preston, standing by the doorway, was pitiful to see, and we unfortunately increased her distress because she was evidently embarrassed to receive guests in her shocked condition and in nightwear hurriedly covered by her heavy winter cloak. Though her beauty clearly shone through her sobbing, tear-stained face and swollen eyes.

I left Mr Beard to comfort her as best he could while I hurried off to fetch the constable. He took an unconscionable time to come to the door, and he grumbled irritably at first; but when I told him of the reason for my calling him out, he dressed quickly and insisted that we collect one of his headboroughs, as his assistants were called.

At length, we arrived at the Prestons' home, where the two officers of the law went through the motions of examining the deceased and asking questions. I did not expect much of them, because I had, only a few years before, seen a production of Shakespeare's *Much Ado About Nothing* in the Drury Lane Theatre in London, and assumed that this Brighthelmston pair would match the Bard's portrayal of Dogberry and Verges.

In fact, Mr Beard told me on our journey home that Mr Wigney was an efficient and conscientious officer and had displayed remarkable courage during the appalling flooding of the town, only three months earlier. He even quoted to me a passage from a book, then just published, about how overworked these officers of the law were. It ran as follows: 'In summer Brighthelmston too frequently becomes the chief receptacle of the vice and dissipation which the sickening metropolis disgorges into our watering places at this season.'

The constable and his men did, in the event, contribute little to the case. But it was a difficult one, as the reader will learn, and I suppose, on mature reflection, that they probably did their best, since, also, they were increasingly busy coping with the raucous escapades of some of the visitors starting to arrive in the town.

In that crowded room of grief, my impatience with the constable made me, if that was possible, pity Mr and Miss Preston even more. Although my mood was a mixture of these thoughts and emotions, my mind was perfectly lucid. It was quite evident to me that I should try to trace the murderer and not leave the investigation solely to these incompetents, as I then impertinently considered them to be. After the constable and his assistant had left, I made my offer to the heart-broken father and sister, an offer they eagerly, gladly and gratefully accepted. We made an arrangement that I should visit them that afternoon (for it was now past midnight). Mr Beard and I then made our way to the cart and so back to Rottingdean.

By now, on the journey, we both wanted to talk. He started: 'I fully accept that it is no excuse,' he said, 'but the reason I stayed so long in 'The Black Horse' is that we were discussing this fearful weather. No one can remember or has heard of such cold. After last autumn's bad harvest and the bitter winter killing so many people, the unseasonable chill as late as May is too much to bear. My crops are blighted and the younger and weaker lambs and even sheep are perishing. Not only that, while we farmers are suffering in these ways, the demands on us as rate payers have doubled over the past year as so many more villagers have become dependent on poor relief. No wonder. Last week I looked into a baker's shop in Brighthelmston and was horrified to see that the price of a quartern loaf has now reached one shilling, such is the effect of the shortage of corn.'

'As a matter of fact,' I said, 'I spent yesterday afternoon talking about these awful conditions with my friend Thomas Hudson; after all, it falls to the clergy to visit the most unfortunate of our parishioners.'

'I think that the most poignant proof of our shortage of food,' continued my companion, 'is the action of the poor wretches now awaiting the gruesome fate meted out to them by the court martial in Brighthelmston.'

Mr Beard was speaking about the mutinous conduct of soldiers of the Oxford militia stationed at East Blatchington to guard the harbour of Seaford, some miles to the east of Rottingdean. In despair and fury over their paltry, bad quality rations, they had broken in to a flour mill, then moved on to the nearby harbour of Newhaven where they boarded a cargo ship and tipped its wheat into the River Ouse. Thirteen were arrested and tried at a court convened at 'The Old Ship' in Brighthelmston. The sentences, announced on 13th May, were that two should be shot, one to be transported and six to be flogged. The floggings were to be between 500 and 1,500 lashes. The people of the town were horrified at the inhumane punishments, they protested and appealed for clemency. Everyone was talking about their fate. Yet the authorities remained unmoved. Accordingly, on 12th June, a fortnight after this conversation with Mr Beard, the men to be shot and flogged were taken to meet their fate at Goldstone Bottom, near the little settlement of Hove; though after a great number of lashes, those who were flogged were reprieved to prevent their dying of this hideous ordeal.

Mr Beard went on to say: 'The mutiny must be seen as well in the context of the tighter organisation and discipline imposed by His Grace the Duke of York since he took command of all the bits and pieces of our disordered army last year. Also, it makes one wonder how secure will the officers' control be over our own summer and autumn military camp. These events will at the very least put a damper on the displays this year.'

These annual gatherings and the accompanying martial parades and mock battles on land in and near Brighthelmston were extremely popular with the town's people and visitors, who arrived in substantial numbers for the spectacles. In addition, the organising of the camp has a minor role in our story.

12

Responding to Mr Beard's comment, I said, 'But the Prince of Wales has no fear visiting us. The Rev Hudson has told me that His Royal Highness and his new wife will be arriving in Brighthelmston very shortly.'

'There is no doubting that Prince George has come to love Brighthelmston over the past few years,' Mr Beard replied. 'Let us hope that Princess Caroline will enjoy the town as much as her husband. Perhaps the magic of the sea will help to make their marriage a happy one.' He added that comment with, perhaps, an optimistic tongue in cheek.

This part of our conversation requires, I own, some explanation. Brighthelmston was already at this time a flourishing fishing town and seaside resort with nearly 400 tradesmen serving the needs of these permanent and temporary populations. Its resident population, burgeoning in this fame, was then ten times that of Rottingdean. There were two main reasons for Brighthelmston's attraction. One was the development of the fashion of 'taking the sea cure' and its consequent rise as a health resort. The other reason was the patronage of members of the royal family, notably the King's eldest son and thus the Heir Apparent to the throne, George, the Prince of Wales; for he rented and later purchased the house which was developed as the Marine Pavilion and somewhat later, when extended, the Royal Pavilion.

Talking to Mr Beard made our way back to Rottingdean seem much shorter than our outward journey, even taking into account the circumstances of that unhappy ride. He set me down at my home. I went to bed, completely exhausted. Sleep soon came, albeit interrupted because I was only too aware that I had the daunting challenge of an investigation into a murder to think about directly I was fully awake.

Chapter 2

I rose late, washed, shaved, dressed, ate breakfast and fed Billy, my ginger feline companion. A normal routine. Except, as I went automatically through this procedure, I became increasingly concerned.

I had given my word that I would find the murderer. Yet, apart from the dying man's clues, I had precious little to go on. Nor had I any experience or expertise to call upon in my endeavours. I posed myself a probing question: by what right did I commit my time and energies to this amateur work – and probably waste them on it – when I had my priestly duty to assist my vicar in caring for the parishioners of Rottingdean? I had not even told (confessed to?) Dr Hooker my, perhaps foolhardy, undertaking.

But my most profound uneasiness lay in my self-doubt: why had I so precipitately made the offer? Was I guilty of the sin of arrogance in believing that I could be more successful than the professional enforcers of the law, however poor my initial judgment of them had been? Even more wounding for my conscience, I began to wonder if my real motive had been much less judicial than amorous. As I was finishing my breakfast – quite oblivious of Mrs Heath's awareness of my distracted mood – I tussled with this last, and most challenging, consideration. My heart pounded in response to the tension between thoughts of guilt and happiness. I prayed, literally prayed to God, that I could be honest with myself.

This act of concentration led to a happy resolution, a bringing together of the two motives into harmonious relationship. I knew, without any measure of doubt that I had fallen in love with Mary Preston. Investigation into her brother's murder would afford me splendidly valid opportunities for seeing her, in order to report the progress of my investigations and to induce in her the deepest gratitude if they proved successful. Yet, I became sure during this self-communing, that the selfish element in my motives strengthened, rather than undermined, my perfectly unselfish determination to help bring to justice the evil perpetrator of Mary's present awful sadness, the heartless and cowardly ambush and murder of her beloved brother.

Who better to assess the honesty of my argument than my vicar? I found him busily grooming one of his horses, but he was exceedingly glad to see me, so anxious was he to be brought up to date. He listened intently as I told him of the night's events, my offer to investigate and the subsequent struggle with my conscience on that matter. Thomas showed no signs of hesitation.

'Do not bother yourself about your parochial duties,' he said, with an encouraging smile, 'I can take over many of these by reducing my riding activities, an arrangement that will salve *my* conscience by feeling that I shall be indirectly helping with the solution of this heinous crime. And, as to your conscience, you are one of the most virtuous and sensitively honest men I know. There, I've said it, and don't look so embarrassed. Get on with this highly beneficent and charitable of civic tasks. You will be acting as a true Christian; and may you be wholly successful!'

I wondered how many men devoid of virtue and honesty Dr Hooker knew, if I rated comparatively so highly in his estimation! Nevertheless, my heart and spirit thus uplifted, I set off for Brighthelmston. As I rode a brisk south-westerly wind blew white-foamed waves on to the beach below the cliffs, a beach strewn with hunks of chalk hacked from the cliff-face by the perennial fierce assaults of the sea.

James and Mary Preston were in their book- and map-stocked shop, each, inevitably, dressed in the black garments of mourning. Both were eagerly awaiting my arrival. And I hoped I detected, as part of the eagerness in Mary's face, a personal pleasure in seeing me.

We withdrew behind the crowded shelves and tables to the parlour at the back of the shop. Besides the normal furniture in that modest accommodation there stood against one wall a trestle table, which bore a coffin containing Jonathan. Those arrangements, Mr Preston told me, were made that morning by Mr Edward Cobby, the hosier and used clothes dealer, but also part-time undertaker and, later, the compiler of the useful little *Brighthelmston Directory for 1800*: a truly versatile man. Mr Preston also asked me if I would be kind enough to attend the funeral the following day, the service to be conducted by my friend, Tom Hudson. (I called him 'Tom' to distinguish him from Thomas Hooker.) Naturally, I thanked him for *his* kindness in inviting me.

I then retailed my experiences of the previous evening, including the words, as far as I could interpret them, which Jonathan had uttered. Inevitably my story caused them great distress. Mary started to cry. I cursed myself for being so thoughtless and callous, and, with some confusion, tried to apologise.

She wiped her tears. 'Of course you had to tell us everything. How otherwise could we help you?' she said with true understanding and gentle firmness. 'Please ask us any questions you think we might be able to answer.'

'The first, I know, is a silly, almost impertinent one,' I said. 'But I must ask it: do you know if Mr Jonathan had any personal enemies? From the little I've heard about him from Mr Beard, I cannot believe that this could possibly be so.'

Mr Preston replied that he was unable to think of anyone who would wish to kill his artist son. Yet he made this statement with a slight hesitation in his voice, stealing the while a rapid glance at his daughter.

'To be fully truthful, Mr Sydenham,' Mary said, 'Jonathan had been unusually quiet during the past few days, as though he was troubled about something. But when father asked him, he said that there was nothing untoward. This was completely out of character. We have been a close family, with no secrets. Mother died when Jonathan and I were quite young, so all three of us had to help each other even more than we might have done if we had had her to rely upon. Jonathan was four years older than me and was especially kind and considerate. Father and I concluded that whatever was worrying Jonathan, he wished to spare us sharing in the problem.'

'Do you think that he might have confided in someone else?' I asked.

'Jane Patcham,' Mary replied without hesitation. 'She and Jonathan were planning to be married.'

Mary had visited Miss Patcham that morning and had left after some time, having been unsuccessful in her tender attempts to console her. Jane was hysterically distraught, hardly to be wondered at.

Mary went on to explain that Jane lived at Marlborough House, the magnificent building on The Steyne, recently thoroughly renovated inside and out, including the cladding of the brickwork with stone. She was employed by its owner, and the instigator of the improvements, the MP Gerald Hamilton, to help look after the house and Mr Hamilton himself, who was in fast-failing health. (In fact, he died a year after the events I am narrating.)

It was evident that I should talk to Miss Patcham; equally evident that that day was out of the question, despite the frustration I felt, because she might well be a vital source for my first enquiries. However, I still had much to talk about with Mr and Miss Preston.

'I shall, of course, see Miss Patcham at the funeral tomorrow,' I said. 'Perhaps you will be good enough to introduce us then, and we can judge when it would be tactful to ask her the questions that I have in my mind to pose. But I am afraid I still have more matters to ask you about, if I may,' I continued, addressing both the bereaved.

'Do please carry on,' said James Preston.

'Well,' I said, 'my next question must be whether you can make anything more of Jonathan's words than the interpretations I have been able to give them.'

'As for me,' Mr Preston admitted, 'I can progress no further than you, Reverend Sydenham. What about you, Mary?'

'Not really,' she said, 'though I think we should talk to Mr Sydenham about Jonathan's prints.'

'I agree,' I said, 'but before we turn to them, I would be honoured if you would call me Ben, and allow me to call you both by your Christian names, for we shall be working closely together on this dreadful business. I beg you not to be offended, and I shall understand perfectly if you feel, at such a brief acquaintance, that this would be too presumptuous.'

James readily concurred. Mary blushed. 'I would be delighted,' she added. And my delight, I am sure, was at least equal to hers. She then said, 'I should explain that, in addition to keeping house for the three of us, I have mounted and framed Jonathan's pictures and kept his accounts. So I have known all that he has produced.'

'Could we,' I suggested, 'perhaps go up to his studio and workshop so that I can provide for myself a kind of mental picture of this work that seems such a cardinal feature in this mystery?'

James acknowledged that this was a capital notion, but that he should stay to attend the shop (and Jonathan's body), while Mary and I went aloft. I must in all honesty confess that the amorous motive for my visit was now in great danger of overshadowing the motive of detection.

The room was meticulously organised. Mary and I sat down while I questioned her about their work. What I especially wanted to know was the number and subject matter of the prints her brother had taken to Rottingdean. As she kept the records of all transactions she was easily able to refer to that day's entry.

She explained: 'Jonathan took five. These were: Marlborough House, the Friends' Meeting House, the theatre and two of the Marine Pavilion. Mr Beard told me last night that he had chosen the Friends' Meeting House because of his family's connection with the Quakers, Marlborough House, and one of the Marine Pavilion. Jonathan and he had agreed a price and I was to mount and frame them as soon as possible. The Marlborough House and both the Marine Pavilion prints were the ones that were stolen.'

I should write a few words now about the Marine Pavilion. The core was a farmhouse owned by a local landowner Thomas Kemp (whose son, by the way, became quite famous as a politician and designer of the recently extended area of Brighthelmston named after him as Kemp Town). Twelve years before the time of my tale, the Prince of Wales started to take summer holidays in Brighthelmston, especially to enjoy the swimming, horse racing and fashionable social gatherings. He soon decided that he would like a residence of his own in the town and arranged for Kemp's house to be bought, and frequently, over the years, to be added to, in oriental decorative and architectural styles. At first he rented the property, before eventually buying it.

To resume my narrative, I said to Mary: 'As all of what your brother had with him was stolen, apart from the prints that were dropped, the most likely explanation for the attack was simply robbery. On the other hand, was there something significant about the assailant's trying to steal the prints? After all, one of Jonathan's dying words suggests that.'

'It seems a bit far-fetched,' Mary replied, puckering her brow. 'There was nothing special about these pictures. Maybe Jonathan's attacker was planning to burgle Marlborough House or the Marine Pavilion with some other criminals and wanted to show them what the buildings look like? Their contents would certainly be extremely valuable. But even this is hardly likely, is it?'

I agreed that all this was not very credible. Besides, how would the murderer have known what Jonathan was carrying in his saddlebag? Yet the question still nagged me: why did Jonathan make such an effort to say that word? At the time, neither Mary nor I could come up with a really sensible explanation.

Except for the inventory and accounts ledger, the contents of the studio and workshop gave no clues. Nor could Mary help immediately with an interpretation of her brother's other words, and she agreed with me that the reference to Dr Hooker, who had no knowledge of Jonathan, was, in the circumstances, disappointing and mysterious. We decided to leave it there, Mary to puzzle over Jonathan's words and for us to talk again – apart from our meeting at the funeral – after I had had the opportunity to speak to Jane Patcham.

As the St Nicholas vicarage was only a few lanes away from the Prestons' home, I decided to visit Tom Hudson before returning to Rottingdean. He was naturally saddened by the violent death of one of his congregation. Once again, I told my story. However, he could only agree with me that the obvious explanation was robbery, which led, without intent, to murder because Jonathan had resisted. And my friend was equally perplexed about the victim's dying words. He agreed to keep his ears open for any gossip about the affair. I bade him farewell, saying I would see him on the morrow at the funeral.

As Betsy took me home I tried to picture the dim outline of the attacker as he rode away from the scene of his crime. To little avail, except I realised that he seemed to disappear behind the coastguard station and cottages at Greenway on the edge of the village of Ovingdean, between Brighthelmston and Rottingdean. During the rest of the day I bought fish for Billy from the Rottingdean fishermen on the beach, reported to Thomas Hooker and visited some of our neediest elderly parishioners, carrying a basket of food for distribution.

The next morning, I went to Brighthelmston for the funeral. A knot of people gathered outside the Prestons' home and eventually we formed a cortège following the coffin. The line of mourners, led by the Rev Hudson, emerged from the congested built-up area and was in due course trudging up the hill, then along the elm-lined avenue through the churchyard to the church. After a brief service inside, we assembled round the grave that had been prepared by the sexton. At one point during the committal I caught a brief glimpse of a man a short distance away, lurking at the corner of the building. I gained the impression that he was intently watching the proceedings. Until, that is, he noticed that I had observed him, when he swiftly disappeared behind the church wall.

The ceremony over and the sexton shovelling the earth on to the coffin, we started to wend our way back down the hill. Mary took this opportunity to introduce me to Jane. I expressed my condolences as best I could; for her part, she thanked me for taking such an interest. She reminded me somewhat of Mary, though her hair was light and her eyes were blue, whereas Mary's hair was dark like her brother's and her large eyes, a dark brown. Also, Jane was a little shorter than Mary, who was quite tall for her sex. Both, I guessed were in their early twenties. I soon came to learn that they each had that sterling quality of refusing to be overcome by adversity.

James made the suggestion that we, together with the few close friends, including the vicar, should congregate in his small parlour for collective remembrances of Jonathan; then, when all the rest had departed, Miss Patcham and I could talk

And so it happened that I came to tell my sad and mysterious tale yet again, this time to the bereaved fiancée.

'You tell me,' she said, 'that, apart from the two discarded prints, all the belongings he had about his person were taken.'

I nodded to confirm.

'Then the murderer must have got away with Jonathan's most treasured possession,' she said. 'This was his chiming watch, with a miniature of myself, which he painted, and was

21

placed inside the hinged cover. I gave it to him as a present.'

She broke down momentarily at the memory. It had taken great courage to tell me that, and the strain of untold grief and repressed anger revealed themselves on her pretty face. Even so, in addition to my compassion, I felt a tinge of excitement. If the murderer was stupid enough to sell the watch and we could trace it, it might lead me to him. And if he kept it, and we found it on him, so much the better! I explained my train of thought to my three companions, as I now considered them.

I then asked Miss Patcham if she felt sufficiently composed to listen to some questions. She said that she was, and, indeed, was anxious to help as much as she was able. I started, naturally, with Jonathan's last words. She explained that Mary had reported these to her, and that she was as baffled as all the others from whom I had sought elucidation.

Treading on more delicate ground, I asked if she had noticed anything different in Jonathan's demeanour recently. Like James and Mary Preston, she hesitated; and, like them, she admitted that he had seemed worried. However, unlike the dead man's father and sister, Miss Patcham was able to elaborate.

It transpired that Miss Patcham's employer, Mr Hamilton, was basically a kindly person and allowed Jonathan to visit Jane – in the presence of the housekeeper, naturally – fairly frequently. Jane explained that it was on one of these visits that he was in a state of some distraction.

'Not many people in this cold weather are brave and committed enough to bathe in the sea,' she said.

I was confused. What on earth had this to do with Jonathan's manner on that day?

Forgive me, dear reader, I am so anxious to write down my narrative at speed that I am prone to forget that it must occasionally be interrupted for crucial explanations. This is indubitably such a juncture.

The sea had become a great attraction. The drinking of sea-water, bathing in sea-water, even breathing 'sea air' were commended as of the utmost benefit to health. This fashion was started in Brighthelmston some half-a-century before the time of my tale.

As readers of this account who have visited seaside health resorts will know – but I include this description for those who do not – bathers enter the sea by means of a vehicle called a 'bathing machine', which, in the 1790s in Brighthelmston, they hired for one shilling per session. The said machine is a hut on wheels, drawn into the water by a horse, in order to preserve the decency of the minimally clad bather when he or she descends from the vehicle to the sea. At Brighthelmston at the time of our story there were four sets of these devices – one set each for ladies and for gentlemen at the west of the town and another pair of sets at the east.

I cannot resist the temptation of quoting from *The New Brighton Guide* (notice the abbreviation of the town's name creeping into use), published a year after the murder. The author was commenting on the failure of the builders of the 'chariots' (as they were sometimes laughingly called) to provide an awning over the steps of the contraptions. I quote the passage to express my disgust at the shameful immorality of the town. The writer explained that the lady bathers 'are all severely inspected by the aid of telescopes, not only as they confusedly ascend from the sea, but as they kick and sprawl and flounder about its muddy margins, like so many Naiads in flannel smocks'.

Disgraceful. But to resume my account: 'I must admit,' I said to Miss Patcham, 'that I can find nothing attractive about this habit and doubt its therapeutic value. I also think the whole ceremony bizarre; though, forgive me, I do not mean to be disrespectful to Mr Jonathan Preston, merely to say that I would not engage in the activity myself. I understand, by the way, that a veritable cohort of helpers are necessary to thrust the participants with hefty vigour into the sea.'

'That is correct,' Miss Patcham confirmed. 'The ladies are attended by "dippers" and the gentlemen by "bathers".

Jonathan became especially friendly with the dipper Martha Gunn after "Smoaker" Miles, the favourite bather, died last year. They were both so saddened by "Old Smoaker's" death, as indeed was the Prince, for it was this great "character" who taught His Royal Highness to swim.'

'I can well imagine anyone striking up a close relationship with Martha Gunn,' I said. 'Even I have heard of her reputation as being a heartily jolly person, with a character as ample as her rotund figure.' (I bit my tongue at this disparaging simile.) 'And I have heard that the Prince is very fond of her. But I don't understand the connection between bathing in the sea and Jonathan's change of mood.'

'Oh, I'm sorry,' Jane apologised. 'It was after one of his bathing sessions that I noticed that he was worried.'

She had mentioned that before, now comprehension of its import dawned. 'In that case, I must talk with Mrs Gunn at the earliest opportunity. She may be able to throw some light on this melancholy affair. I certainly hope so. On a different matter, and I am deeply sorry to fatigue you more with my questioning,' I continued, addressing now all three of the bereaved, 'but did any of you see the man skulking by the church when we were standing by the grave? I caught only a fleeting sight of him; I am sure he feared that he might be seen and recognised. My vague impression is of a person aged about 30 or so, with nondescript hair and clothes. Not very helpful, I'm afraid.'

None of my new friends had seen this person, or could identify him, or explain why a stranger should make a furtive appearance at so very private and solemn an occasion.

Chapter 3

A man with a pistol was lurking around the bathing machines and Martha Gunn was trying to hide from him, her bulky frame making that a difficult endeavour. He shot her dead.

It was the sharp crack of the gunshot – exactly the sound I heard the evening Jonathan was killed – that woke me with such a start from this dream. I was, it goes without saying, mightily relieved to discover that the event I had witnessed was merely imagined in my sleep. I sat up, my heart pounding with the shock.

Almost instantaneously I had a flash of understanding, no doubt spurred into my consciousness by the dream. As Jonathan lay dying in my arms, his first utterance had been the hesitant 'mmm … gun', as I have already reported. Why should he give priority to telling me that he had been shot with a gun when that was transparently obvious? It now came to me that what he was really trying to say was 'Martha Gunn'.

This realisation made it absolutely imperative that I seek her out. Further sleep was impossible. I spent the rest of the night and the early morning in tense impatience until it was time for me to ride to Brighthelmston at an hour when she might be found.

I did, in fact, quickly come across her. She was by no means difficult to recognise: a figure all enveloped in copious clothing topped by a huge hat. I explained my purpose and was comforted and gratified that she was only too ready to talk.

'I'm ever so glad that you're helping and that you've come to see me,' she said. 'Mr Jonathan, he were a splendid feller and so considerate. He wanted to follow the fashion of having his hair cropped, but he didn't so that his bather could haul him out of the water by his queue. I do know why he was worried; he had every good reason to be. When he confided in me about what was troubling him, he pleaded that I should not tell his father or his sister or his fiancée. And he had good reasons too for keeping it all from them – you'll see when I tell you. Directly I heard of his murder, I knew that I should do something, but I couldn't make up my mind what. I shall be ever so relieved now to get it off my chest.'

She spoke quietly, all the while looking round to ensure that no one was overhearing her. We then sat down on a rough seat and she started her story. (I make no attempt to reproduce her Sussex accent.)

'It was last Monday; no, I tell a lie, last Tuesday, that he had a bathe. The weather wasn't quite so cold that day. When he came along to me from the gentlemen's bathing machines he looked as white as a sheet. I'll tell you what had happened.'

It was obvious that she had retained a vivid mental picture of the scene.

'After he had been pulled back to the beach he took a long time drying himself and dressing. No one else was waiting to be done, so he didn't have to hurry and his bather wandered off. Tell the truth, there hadn't been many people wanting us for days and the place was almost deserted – even most of the dippers and bathers had made themselves scarce. The weather's been so bad and it's ever so early in the season for many visitors yet. Mr Jonathan was about to climb down when he heard voices just outside. Something in the way they was talking made him think they was hatching a plot. He also thought they had chosen the empty spot deliberate for their meeting. They'd no idea the bathing machine they was behind was the only one with someone in it!'

Mrs Gunn paused for breath, so fast had she been speaking

in her desire to spill out the whole of her tale. I, of course, was riveted by her report.

She continued: 'There was three men. From what they was saying, Mr Jonathan reckoned that one were a soldier from the camp that is being got ready just over there in Hove; one were a coastguard, though what station he couldn't tell; and the third were a smuggler.'

It was bad enough that such a trio should be meeting in a conspiratorial way. But what the 'queen of the dippers' then went on to report was truly horrifying.

'I'll tell you more or less what Mr Jonathan told me,' she said. 'They really was planning the most dreadful plot. A band of smugglers are going to kidnap the Prince and Princess of Wales when they come to stay here in a fortnight's time. Then they're to take 'em to their hideout over in France. Then they're going to ask for money to give 'em up. Other smugglers will make one of their ordinary landings at Rottingdean and the coastguard in the plot will tell his mates and the excise men about that. So all the preventive officers would be at Rottingdean while the kidnapping band make land at Brighthelmston, and no one to catch 'em. And this is the cunning bit: the soldier will arrange some diversion – exactly what, Mr Jonathan couldn't find out – not only at the camp, but at the two new barracks as well. You know, the one behind 'The King and Queen' (with its handy little hatch to the barrack yard!) and the other up the road that goes to Lewes. The idea is, that, if anyone is able to escape to raise the alarm when the kidnapping happens, it would be difficult to muster any soldiers quickly.'

I was aghast. In my wildest nightmares that I suffered as I intermittently dozed during the night after Jonathan's murder, I had not envisaged anything as treacherous and disastrous as this foul conspiracy.

For once, my mind raced. First – fool that I was – when Jonathan gasped, as I thought, 'prints', what he was in fact saying was 'Prince': he was trying to warn me of the plot.

Also, it seemed, if I now had *this* interpretation correct, then his 'h-hook-er' must indeed be a warning that my vicar, in his capacity as a smugglers' look-out, would innocently and inadvertently, be involved in the plot. Moreover, 'private ... er ... meeting' meant not a private meeting, rather the meeting Jonathan had overheard, but attended by an army private. The mysterious clues were now shaping themselves in my head as a coherent message.

'His worry then was rather like mine now: that is, what to do with this information,' I said. 'The conspiracy is quite evidently well beyond the competence of our constable to cope with.'

'Not just that,' was the dipper's reaction. 'Jonathan naturally started to leave the machine only when he thought the three men was well away. He peered out, and they was in fact a good way off. But, just as he stepped down, one of the civilians, who was carrying his hat, dropped it and bent down to pick it up. As he did this, he turned slightly. Jonathan was scared that he might have been seen. If so, he knew that his life was in peril in the event of the plotters finding out who he was.'

'No wonder,' I said, 'that he kept from his dear ones his fear of the danger he might be in. Also, this provides a really credible explanation for his murder. It was not to rob him, but to silence him.'

I thanked Mrs Gunn profusely and told her that I would go immediately to the Prestons' home to tell them this extraordinary and frightening story, also to think through with them a plan of campaign, then return to tell her how we meant to proceed.

James and Mary were, not surprisingly, utterly shocked by what I had to tell them. We agreed that we at least had some clear understanding about the reason for Jonathan's murder. On the other hand, we all felt overwhelmed by the magnitude and complexity of the planned crime into which we were now being drawn. For, if we had little confidence that the constable, left to his own devices, would be able to solve the murder, we felt that he would be even more out of his depth if faced with tackling this developing treasonous conspiracy. Looking back now, in my mature years, I realise that we should have alerted him and that he would have contacted the appropriate authorities. But at the time we were too emotionally involved to see this.

We therefore settled down to analysing the components of our problem and outlining, on our part, how we could both help prevent the plot from being successfully executed and bring the murderer to justice. We were at one in accepting that our original, self-appointed task was now inextricably entangled in this bigger conspiracy. James Preston produced a sheet of paper to write out our scheme as our discussion clarified our minds.

I started by explaining what I considered to be our central problem. 'I think that, before we list the components of the situation, we should talk about what I believe to be an exceptionally tricky moral and tactical dilemma. It is this. We have, as we have just agreed, two objectives, what we might call the personal and the national. However, in tackling the national one – the kidnapping plot – we may undermine our chances of success in finding Jonathan's murderer – our personal objective.'

James and Mary looked slightly bewildered. I outlined my reasoning. 'It seems to me that the Prince and Princess can be protected in one of two ways. One is for a message to be sent, explaining the danger and stopping their visit to Brighthelmston. The other is that they should come and be protected by an absolutely efficient bodyguard. But either way, we shall almost certainly lose any chance of apprehending the murderer. It appears that he must be one of the conspirators, and when they hear of whichever of these precautionary measures are adopted, they will abort their plan. After all, it would be well nigh impossible to keep secret the alteration of the Prince's established arrangements. The plotters would be confirmed in their suspicions that Jonathan had heard their conversation and, worse, had passed it on. His murderer would then make very sure that he gave no clue to his identity.'

I concluded this exposition by admitting that, so far, in the brief time I had had to ponder the dilemma, I had come up with no solution.

James and Mary looked crestfallen. They grasped the problem immediately and were pessimistic at arriving at a plan that would allow the simultaneous and successful pursuit of both goals.

James was nevertheless persistent and asked, 'Could we even so now do the simple job of writing down the separate elements in this crisis, for such it is?'

We agreed. After much discussion his list was as follows:

1.   Identify the three conspirators.

2.   Take the commanding officer of the camp into our confidence, partly to help identify the soldier-conspirator and partly so that he be forewarned – and could warn the barracks' commanding officers that something unusual and dangerous is to take place.

3.   Explain all to Dr Hooker, partly to warn him about his possible implication in the diversionary landing and partly in the hope that, through his smuggling contacts, he might be able to discover the identity of the smuggler-conspirator and even, if possible, the date when the landing, and therefore the kidnapping, was to take place.

4.   Devise a plan that would ensure the protection of the royal couple, without the conspirators finding out, and choose a person in authority to whom we would put our plan so that it might be set in train.

Although satisfied with the list as a method of elucidating our tasks, it threw us into a condition of despondency. The difficulties were truly forbidding in themselves; surmounting them seemed impossible in the time we had available. Word was about, as Martha Gunn had told me, that the Prince and Princess were arriving in about two weeks. True, the plotters might not arrange, or be able to arrange, to strike immediately on the royal party's arrival. That was little comfort.

We each supplied several ideas, none of which, on close inspection, satisfied our double needs. We must have spent nearly an hour when, Mr Preston occupied with a customer in the shop, Mary exclaimed: 'I think I have it!' Her father came back from the shop and Mary elaborated.

'The first fact we must remember,' she said, 'is that the Prince and Princess and their servants will be staying, not at the Marine Pavilion, which the Prince has been using, but, because it is being decorated, at Marlborough House. I know this because Jane has told me: Mr Hamilton is a friend of the Prince. It is quite possible that the conspirators know this too: they would have taken the precaution of talking to the painters, if nothing else. We must ensure that Their Royal Highnesses do come to Brighthelmston for the reason Ben has argued – that the conspirators should not become suspicious and be frightened off. We must therefore ensure that they are securely guarded in Marlborough House, but without anyone else knowing.'

Neither Mary's father nor I could fault this background to Mary's evolving plan. Yet we looked at each other, both our faces setting into a slight frown. We were having the same niggling, fundamental thought: how were armed guards to be infiltrated into Marlborough House without the plotters finding out what was happening? James asked his daughter this crucial question.

'That's the best part of my scheme,' she said, blushing at her own immodesty.

'Well, don't keep us on tenterhooks,' said I, with impatience, but with unalloyed admiration too.

'It is obvious,' she continued, 'that, during the coming few days, carts and wagons will be arriving with deliveries of all sorts of items that the royal party will need, particularly food, drink and, in this weather, coals. What needs to be arranged, in addition and close to the time of the royal couple's arrival, is for other deliveries – of bags, boxes and crates, containing such items as pistols and swords – to be taken in by carters who are, in fact, soldiers in disguise. But not all these will leave. No one will notice. And by the time that Prince George and Princess Caroline arrive, Marlborough House will be accommodating a platoon of armed guards.'

James and I clapped and hurrahed in appreciation. It was a brilliant, ingenious scheme. Nevertheless, there were still many more details to work out. We therefore went back to James's list.

Identifying the would-be kidnappers was vital, yet we had precious little to go on. I was the obvious one to talk to Dr Hooker about the smuggler; and also to the camp commander about the private, because a visit by a cleric would not arouse suspicion. James and Mary would casually converse with their customers and other acquaintances about the coastguard service to discover if any men were known to have dubious characters. And when I reported to Martha Gunn, I would ask her to do the same.

Then there were the delicate problems of warning the Prince, securing his agreement to keeping to his holiday arrangements, ensuring Mr Hamilton's compliance and co-operation and organising the stationing of bodyguards in Marlborough House.

James asserted firmly, 'It is our duty to approach the Lord-Lieutenant of Sussex both as the person responsible for law and order in the county and as someone who could secure an audience with the heir to the throne; the Prince would hardly agree to see any of us, let alone listen to our story and scheme.'

'Nor would the Lord-Lieutenant,' said Mary. 'I suggest that we ask the advice of Mr Hamilton. Apart from anything else, we can't go ahead without his complete approval. And through my friendship with Jane I have met him.'

Again, Mary had thought of a capital arrangement. Setting it in motion was clearly her task. We concluded, it scarcely needs saying, that we should go about our activities with the utmost despatch. I then left.

My first call had to be on my vicar, though I made a very

brief detour to tell my friend Tom Hudson: I could not keep this matter from him. When I reached Rottingdean, I hoped that Thomas Hooker would not be out that afternoon hunting fox, hare or deer, as he still often did several times a week, despite undertaking some of my duties. As Betsy conveyed me along the familiar cliff-top road, the sea was an uninviting grey, so dense was the cloud. 'If only we could have some summer sunshine,' I thought. But the unseasonal weather was the least of my cares. It crossed my mind how often Thomas Hooker was featuring in this drama. This led me to planning how best to broach the subject of our wish to use him in our plan. Everyone in Rottingdean knew that smuggled goods passed through the village. There had been the famous incident before I took up my curacy when revenue officers seized 71 bags of tobacco and 185 gallon-flasks of spirits. Also, there were the underground systems I have already mentioned. But Thomas and I had never talked about the subject. How could we? The vicar could hardly admit to his curate that he was engaged in an illegal activity, and his curate could not admit to his knowing about it. I now had to breach that wall of discretion.

As Betsy walked at only a sedate pace, I had plenty of time to turn over this quandary in my mind. This led me on to the related matter of the identity of the coastguard-conspirator. I recalled that the preventive services had organised defences against smuggling and the purloining of goods from shipwrecks, along the strip of the coastline immediately to the east of Brighthelmston. These included the customs house of the revenue officers in Rottingdean High Street as the headquarters, with an armoury and underground storage, and cottages nearby for the chief officer and his men. The customs house is a tall slim building, built in 1780. There are, in addition, three coastguard stations with their attendant cottages in the area, at, from east to west, Saltdean, Greenway and Black Rock. It was not far from the Greenway station, the reader will remember, that Jonathan was attacked.

I found Thomas, not in the vicarage, but in the church, a simple structure of nave, tower, chancel and south aisle. There was no one else present, so we sat on a pew at the east end of the aisle, away from the door, in order to have our talk and be able to switch our subject of conversation should we hear anyone else enter.

He listened with great concentration as I detailed the plans we had constructed. After I had completed that part of my report, I paused for his reaction. He remained silent for a minute or two. I felt painfully tense. The silence was complete in the thick-walled church; even the infuriating sound of the sheep did not penetrate. What would Thomas's response be?

'You and the Prestons are absolutely right: this is a dangerous situation; it has to be dealt with swiftly but sensitively, and I congratulate the three of you for devising such a splendid plan. I must, of course, help. I shall try to find out who is the traitor among the smugglers through my contacts with these unconventional trading gentlemen.'

He had admitted it, with a lovely euphemism too! My relief was so obvious that he chuckled. Then his chuckle burst into a hearty laugh.

'It was about time,' he said, 'that I admitted to you this occasional nocturnal activity of mine; and it was about time that you admitted that you knew!'

It was my turn to laugh.

When I left the church, I turned to walk down to the beach at the gap in the cliffs, the gap sometimes used by the smugglers. My purpose was to buy more fish from the boats hauled on to the shingle, competing for space with the bathing machines. The battery of small-calibre cannon sited there, to repel a possible French attack, reminded me of the war and of my need to visit the army camp the next day.

Having eaten his fill that evening – what an appetite that cat had! – Billy settled on my lap, purred, fell asleep and twitched as he dreamed, no doubt, of catching field mice, with which Rottingdean has always been plentifully stocked.

Chapter 4

On 1st February 1793 the French government had declared war on Great Britain. This was nearly four years after the outbreak of the French Revolution. From the extraordinarily dramatic fall of the Bastille in July 1789, incredible events occurred with incredible speed. Moreover, with this acceleration came mounting violence: the outbreak of war between France and the two great German states, Austria and Prussia, the execution of the King and Queen, civil war and the period of government-devised bloodshed known as the Terror.

By the summer of 1795, when we uncovered the plot against the Prince of Wales, Britain was being deeply affected in many ways by the Revolution and the war. French spies were operating in the south of England. Refugees, referred to by the French word *émigrés*, fled across the Channel, a number making landfall at Brighthelmston. On the high seas, the navy engaged in numerous operations – battles, convoying, and blockade of the continental coasts. Yet, despite the strength of our fleet, there was constant fear of a French invasion or, at the least, cross-Channel raids. It was becoming a bitterly felt conflict, more intense than the many previous wars between the old adversaries, for Britain was fighting not just a country but also its revolutionary republican ideology.

We were very conscious of the potential peril of coastal raids, as the artillery at Rottingdean reminded us. Military preparations in Brighthelmston, however, were on a far bigger scale than in our village. Two formidable artillery emplacements had been constructed in 1793, to the east and west of the town, the former containing a battery of four 36-pounders and the latter, eight. Moreover, as Mrs Gunn had mentioned to me, two years later, the year of my story, an infantry barracks was built, only about 200 yards north of Marlborough House where the Prince and Princess were to stay and – if our plan came to fruition – were to be guarded; and a second, bigger barracks, for cavalry, was developed further north, about a mile from Marlborough House.

And then there was the camp of regular soldiers, militia and volunteers, whither I was going to talk to the officer in charge. These camps, to which I have already alluded, were started in the summer of 1793 and became annual affairs, involving thousands of troops encamped, from 1794, on land to the immediate west of the town of Brighthelmston, in the large but scantily populated parish of Hove.

En route to the camp I stopped to see Martha, and apprised her of our plans. I knew she would not dream of telling anyone else, and would be alert to gather any scraps of gossip or information: she would be totally committed to looking after the Prince of Wales, who, because of his enjoyment of swimming, had befriended her.

I would not be impertinent enough to try to describe the army encampment better than Miss Jane Austen. In her entertaining novel, *Pride and Prejudice*, which she started to write the year after the tense year of my chronicle, she has her character Lydia seeing 'all the glories of the camp – its tents stretched forth in beauteous uniformity of lines, crowded with the young and the gay, and dazzling with scarlet'. At the time that I am recording, the full camp had not yet been established. A forward party was making preparations, such as marking out the areas for the baggage wagons, the grass roads between the future rows of tents, the cook-houses and the latrines. The captain in charge of this contingent and a few subalterns were already installed, setting up a command headquarters, drawing up plans for the various training exercises, organising the supply of foodstuffs and, I am sure, many other essential preliminary tasks for the smooth running of such a huge undertaking.

As I entered the site the small contingent of troops were at their ease in their tents, though no doubt polishing their brasses and boots! The men of one squad were lustily, though not altogether tunefully, singing the new military march and song that had just become so popular, 'The Girl I Left Behind Me', sub-titled 'Brighton Camp'. When I came within earshot they had reached the second verse. I heard:

… When first she vowed to love me.
But now I'm bound to Brighton camp;
Kind Heaven, then pray guide me,
And bring me safely back again
To the girl I left behind me.

I walked on, unchallenged, to the really large tent. I entered, and was then politely asked my business by the officer in charge. I replied that the matter I needed to discuss was urgent and very confidential. The captain looked doubtful, hesitated, but, probably because of my clerical attire, he said he would listen. I gave him my name and the parish in which I held my appointment; then I was ushered behind a canvas flap.

He was the epitome of a committed and efficient army officer (not all were either!): lean, upright and dressed in an immaculate uniform. He offered me a chair in front of his table, he sat in his, and, having been invited to state my business, I launched into my story.

I started by saying that the problem I wished to put before him was both serious and complicated. Believing that the military mind would appreciate at first a clear, crisp outline, I tried to give him a synopsis, explaining that I would, of course, fill in what few details I had in response to any questions he might pose. I stressed that what we desperately needed was the identity of the fomenter of the planned distraction among the military personnel.

The further I progressed into my narrative, the graver his face became. At least it was evident that he was tending to believe me.

'This is a devilish to-do,' he said. 'I must tell you that I'm not happy with the discipline and mood in this camp already, despite the small numbers so far. The outburst at East Blatchington, and the reaction of the people of Brighthelmston to the court martial here, have made me even more concerned. There's dry tinder here, and it only needs someone like your private-conspirator with prospect of financial reward for igniting it, for the camp to go up in some conflagration, or at least ruining the chances of a harmonious camp when all the units arrive. Though, to be more optimistic, I have been hoping that the stern sentences passed on those East Blatchington mutineers would have a deterrent effect. Oh, my apologies, Reverend Sydenham, for the flowery language, but I'm sure you must sympathise with my realisation now that I must be even more alert.'

I offered him my sympathy. It was very real.

The captain then took out the lists of those troops already in the camp. He scanned the names with their helpful annotations and came up with about a dozen who he thought could be our conspirator because they had already been marked as troublemakers. He said he would ask his trustworthy non-commissioned officers to be aware of any whispers of disaffection or plotting, and to advise him of any clues they might pick up about our man. In turn, he suggested that James and I should patronise 'The King's Head' and 'The George' inns in West Street in the evening, these being the favourite haunts of the men under his command, because they were closest to the camp site.

He concluded by saying that he must send one of his subalterns to summon the colonel who would be the commanding officer once the camp was fully functioning. He, the captain (who would then be the adjutant) held much too junior a rank to handle this advancing crisis himself. He added, to my relief, that he would not reveal to this messenger the nature of the problem and would make him swear not to tell anyone else that he was departing on a special, top secret mission, but to say he was having to sort out an administrative bungle. I was to return several days later to meet the colonel.

In the meantime, as I discovered when I arrived at the Preston household, Mary had already visited Marlborough House. She had, naturally, told her father what had transpired. We went into the parlour and she repeated for me the results of seeing her bereaved friend and her employer. In the absence of her father in the shop, I confess, my bounden duty and my burgeoning passion vied for control of my concentration. Summoning up the Stoic fragment of my character, I listened attentively.

'Jane was pathetically pleased to see me,' Mary said. 'She's still devastated by Jonathan's death. I told her the outlines of our plan and the utmost need of Mr Hamilton's co-operation. So she went to ask if I could talk to him about a serious matter. She was away some time. That did not bode well. Then, after she had returned, we still had to wait in the wonderfully decorated hall and we grew increasingly nervous. At last, Mr Hamilton came slowly from the library, where, as I learned later, he was working on his book, *Parliamentary Logic*, and invited us in to that elegantly appointed room.

Mary then outlined the conversation: '"Now then, young ladies," he said, once we were all seated round a small table. "What have you to tell me?"'

I have no doubt that Mary used all her considerable powers of charm, firmness and command of the detail we had gathered so far to win over the elderly MP.

'It was hard going,' she said. 'I think what made him reconsider his initial assessment that our story was, at best, "exaggerated misunderstanding", to use his own phrase, was my repeating that you are a friend of the Rev Hudson, and that *he* had no hesitation in believing your story.'

What a blessing, I thought, that the Anglican clergy still have some standing in this country, despite the growth of the new Methodist movement, a development which suggests at the very least, some discontent with, even disapproval of, the Established Church. And what a blessing, too, that I had called to see Tom the previous day and that he had accepted the extreme likelihood of a plot being hatched.

At any rate, the outcome of the ladies' appeal was that Mr Hamilton was willing to allow the Prince, suitably protected, to be used as a lure for the conspirators provided that His Royal Highness agreed to that course of action. He advised us that the approach to the Lord-Lieutenant should be made by the Member of Parliament for the eastern portion of Sussex, the Rt Hon Thomas Pelham, who, by good fortune, was also Deputy Lieutenant, and consequently responsible for law, order and security in the Brighthelmston area. It was arranged that Mr Hamilton (who was MP for Haslemere in the County of Surrey) should write a letter to Mr Pelham and that I should take it to him and recruit him to our cause.

'I have only just thought,' Mary said: 'Mr Hamilton was obviously torn between making a fool of himself with the Prince if our story had no foundation, and being culpably negligent if our story was true, the royal couple were kidnapped and he had ignored the warning.'

I agreed with her, and congratulated her most warmly on her persuasive powers, especially her presence of mind in emphasising that my friend Tom believed the plot to be only too real. That comment gave me another thought – but, of that, later.

It was my turn to report the outcome of my visit to the camp. I therefore asked James if he could leave the shop for a while to join us in the parlour. The vital point, of course, was the captain's advice that James and I should take liquid refreshment at the inns frequented by the soldiers of the encampment, and that, out of the dozen hostelries in

Brighthelmston at that time, he was able to specify the two that were popular with the least reputable of his men.

James and I tossed a penny coin. He won, and chose to attend 'The George'; I consequently took 'The King's Head' for that evening. Moreover, James gave me prudent advice to wear non-clerical clothes. How wise! We arranged to compare our experiences and findings, if any, the next morning.

The new thought I had as a result of Mary's skilful use of Tom Hudson's name meant that his vicarage was my next port-of-call.

The reader will not be surprised that he welcomed me most amiably and was quite unable to hide his impatience for my news. I brought him up to date – hurriedly, for I also was impatient.

'Tom,' I said, 'when Jonathan was buried, I caught a glimpse of a man furtively watching the graveside ceremony. Neither James nor Mary nor Jane saw him, not to be wondered at, given their grief-stricken state. Nor would you, since you were conducting the service and had your back to where I fleetingly noticed him. You must admit his presence and behaviour – he rapidly disappeared when I looked up – were suspicious.'

Tom said instantaneously: 'The sexton.'

'No,' I said, 'it was not he, he was near the grave the whole time.'

Tom explained that he meant the sexton might have seen the lurking man. 'That's a good idea,' I said. 'I know it's unlikely, but he might be able to describe him much more clearly than I.'

We went immediately up to the church and found that industrious church employee, the sexton, conscientiously and carefully removing weeds from around the gravestones. He greeted me courteously; I explained my presence.

'I remember the man,' he said, 'and not just because his manner seemed so strange.'

'Could you describe him?' I asked.

'He was dressed very ordinary,' was his disappointing reply. 'But, as I've just said, I had another reason for remembering him.'

'Yes, yes,' I said with impolite curtness, urging him on.

'Well, it were real strange. When the church clock struck the hour – and I keep it in good condition,' he said with pride, 'the man chimed as well!' He looked at us with a face of strained perplexity.

'What a magnificently observant man you are,' I said in genuine appreciation.

The sexton stared open-mouthed at me, as puzzled by my outburst as he had been by the stranger's imitation of the church clock. Tom, too, raised a bewildered eyebrow at me.

Not wishing to reveal too much to the sexton, I said that all we had to do now was to look for a chiming man, thanked him again and pulled Tom away, leaving the poor man scratching his head.

However, I quickly enlightened Tom. 'When Jonathan was murdered,' I said, 'one of the items stolen from him was his chiming watch, which he cherished, not just for its own sake, but because Jane gave it to him. Your sexton obviously has no idea that such things exist; hence his bewilderment. Our mystery man must be wearing that watch. After all, they are not at all common, and it is too much of a coincidence that there should be two in this case. So that man is almost certainly the murderer.'

I left Tom at his vicarage, went to tell my latest news to James and Mary, then to where I had tethered Betsy, and thence back to Rottingdean. Having partaken of a meal I undertook some of my neglected duties in the parish until it was time to return to the Brighthelmston inn.

Attired in clothes that would not declare my priestly vocation, I entered 'The King's Head'. How unlike the atmosphere I was used to in Oxford and Rottingdean! The crowds in the bar looked impenetrable, the air, densely clogged with tobacco-smoke and nauseously reeking bodily sweat, felt unbreathable, and the fortissimo noise seemed to render normal conversation impossible.

Stopping just a little way inside the door, to take stock of these offensive conditions and hazards to acquiring any hints about the murderer and conspirators, I mentally dissected the noise into its components. It comprised, cacophonously: the alcoholically-enhanced shrieks of 'ladies' of, indubitably, easy virtue; the equally inebriated roars of bawdy laughter in the tenor and bass registers of the civilian and military male clientele; and the raucous sounds of gratingly rendered songs, consisting of vocally and instrumentally generated notes produced with little musical sensitivity. This last source of noise I detected, through the auditory competition of shrieks and laughter, was coming from a group of soldiers in a corner, singing the inevitable 'Rule Britannia', 'The Girl I Left Behind Me' and some salacious ditties, evidently highly entertaining to the soldiery, but, I hasten to assure the reader, completely unknown and indeed offensive to me. The male voices were accompanied with, I must admit, some technical expertise, by a concertina and a fiddle.

Uncongenial as I found this environment, I reminded myself of the vital importance of my investigating every possible source of further clues. The compactness of this imbibing crowd required me to discard my natural civility, and elbow my way through the throng in order to purchase a pint of ale, without which I might just as well have appeared in the full regalia of the Archbishop of Canterbury, for all the effort I had made to look like a normal frequenter of the inn.

Equipped with this essential accessory, I gradually moved through the mass of humanity, my ears pricked for any normal talking. I discerned some scraps, mainly gossipy complaints about officers, sergeants and corporals from private soldiers, and about wives, from no doubt unsympathetic and unfaithful husbands. A third theme was the expression of bitter hatred of the French. And I soon discovered that that topic was being aired in 'The George' as well.

There was little point in my staying in 'The King's Head'. *My* head was swimming with the unaccustomed intake of alcohol and the ear-splitting racket. I pushed my way into the street and fresh air. Only to be confronted with more noise a few yards down the road. Some men were spilling out of 'The George', punching and kicking each other and yelling at the tops of their voices. Squeezing past them out of the doorway, looking decidedly frightened, was James. I hurried to help him extricate himself from the *mêlée*.

My use of that French word is deliberate, as being apt for that fracas (I show off with words when I get a chance!). Let me explain.

The war on the continent was dying down. The French now controlled the Low Countries: the Austrian Netherlands had been incorporated into the French Republic, and the United Provinces, renamed the Batavian Republic, were only nominally independent. Peace negotiations were under way in Basle, in Switzerland, Prussia having already signed terms to end its conflict with France. Austria and Russia were losing their appetite for war.

All this meant that Britain was almost alone in maintaining a condition of effective fighting against France. The question therefore arose: should Britain continue? Men were being recruited into the army and press-ganged into the navy, taxes and rates were ruinously high, and the poor were suffering desperately. Pitt was a fine Prime Minister in many ways, but shouldn't he change his priorities? On the other hand, most British people, as was evident from the snatches of conversation I heard in 'The King's Head', looked upon the French with an intense loathing that demanded the continuation of the war, whatever the price.

How were these two opposed arguments to be resolved? The patrons of 'The George' that evening had found a ready answer: fisticuffs.

It was James who explained that this was the origin of the outburst of violence, between civilians and soldiers of each of the two policy persuasions. Two corporals inside 'The George', reinforced shortly by two others from 'The King's Head', were pulling the combatants apart and threatening the soldiers involved with punishment if they did not return to camp.

I walked with James to his home a few lanes away. I told him that I had discovered nothing. He, in his turn, thought that our evening had been wasted.

'There was one curious sight, though, before and just as the fighting started,' he said. 'I was in a corner, so that I could survey the whole room, and close to me was a private, talking in low tones to two civilians. One of these sounded as though he had a French accent. When the quarrelling broke out he looked very frightened and I wondered, given such hatred of the French, why a British soldier should be talking to an ordinary Frenchman, because he didn't appear to be an aristocratic *émigré*. At any rate, the three of them made a quick move to escape. As they were leaving, the English civilian failed to avoid a badly aimed fist intended for someone else. He will have a colourful cheekbone for several days now!'

'Not a wasted evening at all!' I said in some excitement. 'Supposing this: the soldier is 'our' private; the Englishman is the fellow who was lurking in the churchyard; and they have recruited a Frenchman to their conspiracy?'

'Possible,' said James. 'And that means we should return tomorrow evening, both of us, to 'The George' so that if any of them are there again, I can point them out to you. However, two thoughts cross my mind. Jonathan had overheard three Englishmen; there were only two in the inn this evening, so where's the other one? And, the purpose of our going tomorrow is to catch sight of the conspirators. I only hope they haven't noticed me this evening and would be able to recognise me!'

Chapter 5

I woke late the next morning: the effects of my experiences the previous evening? Was the worry of making such slow progress in tracking down the conspirators – now probably four – beginning to tell? We had no names, still less, any exact idea what we would do even when we did know them.

Nevertheless, there were several useful ways for me to occupy myself that day before James and I visited 'The George' in the evening. I had to call at Marlborough House, not only to meet Mr Hamilton and acquire the letter of introduction and support to take to Mr Pelham, but also to tell Jane about the watch. I should also let Martha Gunn know our latest news. Pondering on this list, I wondered if perhaps Mary would accompany me to Marlborough House? I therefore called on her first, explained where I was going, and she gladly agreed to accompany me.

Arriving at Mr Hamilton's house, we were invited in by his youngish manservant, who led us to the magnificent drawing room where the MP was sitting. Mary introduced me. He looked awkwardly guilty and confessed that he had not written the letter to Mr Pelham, mumbling something about pressing personal business. I, with what politeness I could muster, suggested that the safety of the heir to the throne and the apprehension of dangerous criminals were somewhat pressing matters also. He shuffled off.

I later learned that he was notoriously lazy as a Member of Parliament, making but a sole contribution to debates in his entire career in the House of Commons, hence his sobriquet, 'One-Speech Hamilton'. However, to be fair, it was also suggested that his silence had been bought by a government fearful of his hostile views. Also, in exoneration of his laxness concerning the letter, it must be remembered that he was at this time quite ill. At least he was now shamed into sitting down at his desk to write.

While he was thus occupied, Mary and I found Jane and told her the sexton's tale, Mr Preston's observations of the evening before and our plans for the coming evening.

At long last Mr Hamilton produced the letter. I thanked him. Mary and I left, she to return home, I to call on Mr Pelham. Then later, I was to join Mary again to go to see Martha Gunn.

The Rt Hon Thomas Pelham, a relative of the Duke of Newcastle, lived in the Pelham family house at Stanmer, only a little way up the road leading from Brighthelmston to Lewes. It is an elegant, Palladian-style building made of pale yellow sandstone, set in a pleasant park, with its own old church and new cottages. Mr Pelham was in that year aged 39 and had a widespread reputation of being an efficient, friendly and kindly person. As Betsy took me up the avenue, from the road to the house, I was eagerly looking forward to meeting him.

What is more, everything seemed to bode well for his co-operation. Not only because of his character but also because, as Mr Hamilton had told me, he had just, in March of that year, been appointed a Privy Councillor. His support for our plans would consequently carry considerable weight. Betsy seemed to like the setting too – no trying hills for her old limbs.

A pleasant footman, of natural, not artificial politeness I gauged, opened the door and enquired of my business. I gave him my name, explained that I had come to seek Mr Pelham's help on the advice of Mr Hamilton and that the problem was expounded in the letter, which I handed to him. I was invited into a room to wait while the man conveyed the fact of my presence and the letter to his master.

It took only a minute or two for Mr Pelham to appear and take me to his library. He bade me be seated, called for wine, and posed the questions that had come into his mind as a result of reading his fellow-MP's missive. They were penetrating queries – His Majesty, I thought, was fortunate to have a councillor with such a lucid and acute mind as Mr Pelham's. The discussion was interrupted by the arrival of a decanter of fine light wine.

'Forgive my abruptness,' he said, when he was satisfied that he fully understood all aspects of the case, 'but your clear answers have allowed me to come to a conclusion. It is this: I agree with your assessment of the situation and I judge the plan, which you and your friends have concocted, is a darn foxy one and deserves to be put into effect. And I don't need to tell you that there's not an hour to lose. You may not know, but the office of Lord-Lieutenant is currently held by His Grace, the Duke of Richmond, who lives at Goodwood House, between Arundel and Chichester. I shall now prepare to make the journey to him and you may be assured that I shall inform you of the outcome immediately on my return.'

I thanked him profusely for his conviction and support, and took my leave.

I rode directly to the place where I had chosen to tether Betsy for my visits to the Prestons. She was a most canny beast – she took me there herself. I made my way to the shop and explained to James and Mary the success of my visit to Stanmer. They were, it goes without saying, delighted. I then reminded Mary of our arrangement to see Martha Gunn and was forward enough to suggest that, if she had time, we might take a stroll along by the sea. Although the weather was cold, at least the air was still. Mary asked her father's permission, turning sadly to me to say that because she now had few of Jonathan's prints left to mount and frame she had more free time than hitherto.

As we walked, I started by asking her about Jane.

'She has had a dreadfully sad life,' said Mary. 'Her father served in the army and was killed at the Battle of Bunker Hill in the American War of Independence when she was only ten years old. Her mother died of congestion of the lungs five months ago in the appalling winter. Immediately after her mother died she met Jonathan. This made her doubly contented. She had been worried by a man with amorous intentions for some time – she never told me his name – and her attachment to Jonathan gave her a good reason for rejecting these unwanted advances. She was so happy with Jonathan. After all her personal misfortunes, even though a kindly aunt and uncle have been a great help to her, she really thought that her life had changed to prospective happiness.

Mary then asked me about my family. 'Nothing much to tell, really,' I said. 'Until I came to Rottingdean, I lived most of my life in Oxford. My father is a college fellow, teaching Greek and Latin. My mother supplements his income by giving pianoforte lessons. I have a brother and two sisters, though one other brother died at birth and another when he was a few months old.'

'Do you know any other parts of the country or much of Sussex?' Mary asked.

'I am particularly fond of an uncle and aunt who live in Richmond on the Thames river,' I replied. 'I have often stayed with them and they developed my taste for plays. They have taken me to the Drury Lane and Covent Garden theatres. Otherwise, my knowledge of our land is miserably limited. I have not even, I must admit, explored the fair county of Sussex.'

'My father and I must remedy that when our present sad business is over,' my companion said. 'I'm sure you would be fascinated by Chichester Cathedral, for example, with its strange bell-tower separated from the building itself. But, as you are interested in drama, you must have attended the theatre here in Craggs Lane, or Duke Street, as it is now called, which Mr Cobb took over last year, though I can't remember seeing you there. It specialises in new works. For example, last summer father and I attended a highly enjoyable production announced as 'a new Grand Musical, Historical, Pantomimical Entertainment, called *Mary Queen of Scots*'. Though, scarcely the standard of Mr Sheridan's plays, I own!'

'No, I haven't even managed that, I'm afraid,' I said. 'Since coming to Rottingdean last autumn I've been so busy getting to know all our parishioners. Not only that, I wouldn't like to sit alone watching a play; a visit to a theatre should be a friendly, social occasion, and I have not met anyone whom I could join to attend a performance.'

'You have met someone now, though, whom you could accompany, haven't you? You must come with us when the theatre reopens in July,' said Mary, her cheeks glowing a deep pink.

'I am extremely glad that I have,' I said, with equal feeling. 'And what of your family,' I hastily asked, changing the subject in order to curtail our shy embarrassment.

'Well,' she said, 'as you can tell from my surname, my father's family originally came from the village of Preston, you know, just north of Brighthelmston. However, for many generations they have been farmers in Hove. My father was not interested in that kind of life, even though he inherited the sturdy physique for the work. As a boy he showed a preference for leather-bound books over woollen-clad sheep, gathering information rather than gathering wheat. His father taught him to read, using the big family Bible. The vicar of the disgracefully neglected, almost tumbledown church of St Andrew's discovered this bent and encouraged it by lending my father books from his own library.'

'So the fact that you live in a book shop,' I said, 'is no accident.'

'He loves it,' she said; 'but it was, in a way, a lucky chance that he came to own it. My mother was the daughter of a lawyer, always struggling against poverty, who lived in Hove and handled the landowners' legal matters in that area. An unmarried cousin, older than her and whom I called Uncle

Jonah, started our shop, though it attracted precious few customers. After my father and mother were married Uncle Jonah arranged that father should visit the shop. The elderly bibliophile and the young farmhand, plainly unsuited to his job, became great friends. When Uncle Jonah died, my father has told me that he was torn between a bitter sadness at his departing and a happy and totally unexpected gratitude that the old man had left the shop in his will to him.

'I can understand your father's divided feelings,' I said, 'but Uncle Jonah must have passed away content that, by willing the shop to your father, he was doing the greatest of favours to both the shop and his young friend: the shop, after all, gained a caring owner, and this new owner was released from the drudgery of his uncongenial occupation.'

'Even so,' said Mary, 'it hasn't been easy for us to make a living because of the competition of the two big libraries-cum-bookshops in The Steyne, which attract the fashionable visitors in the summer. So father has specialised in stocking maps and foreign books, and, of course, most recently poor Jonathan's prints. The competition from the other shops is especially worrying in these times because the war has interfered with the supply of our French, German and Italian books, and now Jonathan is suddenly no longer with us to produce his pictures. Still, we do have some savings, and our sales of the stock we have of French books have flourished since the arrival of the *émigrés*, who, naturally, could not bring their own libraries with them when they fled. Unfortunately, we have sold all our copies of M. Laclos' risqué *Les Liaisons Dangereuses*!'

Mary blushed as we both laughed at this economic implication of lascivious literary tastes.

She then continued: 'Father encouraged Jonathan and me to take our education seriously; we attended the little free William Grimmet school. Jonathan showed a flair for drawing and painting. And just as one relation helped father to develop *his* interest, so, most fortunately, another relative of my mother's, a talented artist and craftsman, taught Jonathan the skills of etching and printing and me, those of mounting and framing.'

'Do you share your father's passion for literature, by any chance – apart from drama, that is?' I asked.

'Yes,' she replied, 'I enjoy reading when I have the time. I know it is almost dangerous these days to admit it, but I am particularly keen on modern radical political works. I judge that Thomas Paine's *Rights of Man* is a magnificent, cogently argued book. I think it's extraordinary that so many people in this country fear that his ideas could lead England to repeat the horrors of the French Terror when Mr Paine himself was imprisoned for a year in Paris because of his opposition to that violence!' She paused, obviously wondering what my reaction would be. Then she asked: 'Are you shocked?'

I smiled. Mary obviously thought and felt deeply about the problems of our age of terrible misery and violence. I admired her for it and told her so.

She allowed herself to smile too, a charming broad grin, and said, 'In that case, I can make another confession. At the moment I am reading Mary Wollstonecraft's *Vindication of the Rights of Woman*. There! What do you think of that?'

We both laughed once more – with gusto. I admitted that I had no taste for that kind of literature, but understood its appeal to others because of the gross injustices suffered by so many, women included.

'So, Ben, what do you read?' she riposted. It was my turn.

'I continue to study theology, of course, partly because it's my job and partly because I am genuinely interested in the depths and complexity of the Christian religion. My "leisure" reading, if I can call it that, is in the field of science. Not the difficult sciences, involving advanced Mathematics, such as the extraordinarily brilliant work of Isaac Newton, which are beyond my comprehension, but Natural History and the new science of Geology. My most treasured possession is the set of M. Buffon's *Natural History* in its English translation.'

'I know little of these learned researches, though my father has talked to me about them,' Mary said. 'Are you not worried that they conflict with the Bible, the Book of Genesis, that is?'

I admitted that this was a serious problem. 'In some moods,' I said, 'I fear that my scientific reading will damage my faith; in which case the conviction of my priestly ministry will be weakened, even my soul imperilled. Then, in different moods, I feel intellectually challenged, trying to resolve the apparent contradictions. And did you know,' I said, to lighten the conversation, 'that in Paris before the Revolution, some ladies led the discussions on science in their *salons*? You can add that to the arguments for the recognition of women's position in society that you are gleaning from Miss Wollstonecraft!'

We enjoyed the humour together, happily exhilarated in the friendship of our conversation, in learning about each other and our budding relationship.

By then we were approaching the beach, and were aiming our footsteps in the direction of the ladies' bathing machines, in search of Martha Gunn.

She was, surprising in view of the weather, attending to a courageous lady bather. We kept a discreet distance. After the 'ceremony' the dipper came up and greeted us both.

'I'm sorry, but I've not seen anyone matching the description of the three Mr Jonathan overheard and caught a brief sight of,' she said. 'And I haven't heard any gossip that would help.'

'Please don't apologise,' I said. 'It's not all that likely that anything would come your way. It was an extraordinary chance that Jonathan heard what he did. But we have some news for you.'

I told the dipper about the sexton hearing what was assuredly Jonathan's watch, about James seeing two Englishmen, one a soldier, conversing with a Frenchman in 'The George', and about the civilian Englishman receiving a hefty punch.

Martha's eyes lit up. 'That's progress,' she said excitedly. 'This is what I think. The man with Mr Jonathan's watch and the man with what will by now be a lovely coloured cheek must be one and the same person, and he's the murderer. Not only that, but it makes sense that a Frenchman is part of the plot because the kidnappers would take the Prince and Princess to a smugglers' lair across the Channel and would be working with a friend there.'

'I am certain you are right,' I said. 'Thank you. And you've given me another idea. If the party landing at Brighthelmston includes Frenchmen and is a band of ruffians not all of whom are familiar with the town, that would explain the theft of the prints of Marlborough House and the Marine Pavilion from Jonathan's satchel. The three English conspirators may have discovered that it was uncertain whether the Marine Pavilion would be ready in time for the royal couple. The pictures could have been given to the Frenchman, who would have been told later, when it was known, which of these very different-looking buildings would be the holiday home of Their Royal Highnesses.'

'That must be the explanation,' Mary almost shouted. 'And that's one more mystery solved!' I hoped so.

Betsy conveyed me back to Rottingdean, where I called on Thomas Hooker. He told me that he had been given a little hint that day.

'I have been chatting in a nonchalant manner to my friends, the nocturnal importers,' he said.

I enjoyed another judicious euphemism, no doubt based on the popular term for some smugglers as 'owlers'.

'I have gathered that there is one among them who suffers from the sin of avarice and whom the rest do not entirely trust. I have gleaned no name, and, of course, I must proceed with the utmost delicacy and caution. But this man might be our conspirator, don't you think?'

I eagerly concurred.

That evening I met James in 'The George'. We arrived separately so as not to give the impression that we had met by arrangement and sat, talking quietly, drinking abstemiously and observing keenly for some time. None of the three men whom James had seen the previous evening appeared. We decided that there was no point in staying. However, as we pushed our way to the door, we heard a cluster of soldiers talking about the brawl, which James had witnessed, and how a number of their companions were confined to the camp for a week because of their involvement in the violence. It seemed likely that 'our' private was one of these, and that was the reason for our visit being unproductive.

I started the next day on my parochial visits. In the afternoon, as I was leaving one of the cottages, a man approached me. It was Mr Pelham. The Deputy Lieutenant did not look happy. It was evident that he had sought me out for an urgent reason. He came straight to the point.

'Mr Sydenham,' he said, 'we need to talk about the matter of Their Royal Highnesses.'

I led him to my home. Once seated, he explained his worry, with admirable clarity.

'I have been driven post-haste to tell you of my meeting with the Lord-Lieutenant,' he said. 'After much thought and discussion, and not without reservations, he agreed to support your plan in the following manner. His Grace has instructed me in my capacity of Deputy Lieutenant to design arrangements for the selection of a small unit of troops to perform guard duties in Mr Hamilton's house and for their surreptitious introduction into the building.'

'That is capital news,' I said. 'So why your gloom, sir? Is it caused by the matter of his securing the agreement of the Prince to this subterfuge?' I asked.

'It is,' he replied. 'The Duke has instructed the two of us to visit the Prince to apprise him of what you have discovered, to expound the plan and to persuade him to collaborate.'

I gasped, but uttered no words.

'The reasons for this decision are as follows,' he said. 'In the first place, the Lord-Lieutenant's responsibility is to keep watch on developments here, particularly in the light of the uncertain and resentful temper of the local soldiery, so he cannot make the journey himself. Secondly, you know more about the plot and your own plan than anyone else. And thirdly, His Grace has given me a letter explaining his compliance with the plan and commending it to His Royal Highness. Accordingly, we must set out at first light tomorrow. You come to my house, and we shall go to London in my landau.'

He then left. There was no doubting his private pleasure at having been drawn into this affair so fully. No, 'pleasure' is not an apt word: he was as distressed as anyone would have been at the threat to the Prince and Princess. Yet it was clear to me that he would have been unhappy to be excluded from our arrangements. I was relieved at that, yet felt considerable trepidation about my own position. Despite the Lord-Lieutenant's letter and Mr Pelham's support, I doubted that the Heir Apparent would give much credence to a tale told by a poor, young curate with no experience of the world. Still, I had refused to leave the Brighthelmston constable to handle the case, and I had to see through the implications of my arrogance.

I saddled up Betsy to make my way to Brighthelmston yet again; this time by the bridleway across the Downs and fields, so that I could ignore the dark, unattractive sea. I had to tell James and Mary of this latest development. On my return, I also visited Dr Hooker. Then to bed, to attempt as much sleep as I could in my perturbed state.

Chapter 6

Mr Pelham had suggested that we make the journey to London in his carriage rather than on horseback, because we needed to look presentable for our audience with the fashion-conscious Prince; we could pack extra clothes in the vehicle. In any case, Betsy could not possibly have made the 54 miles along the shortest of the routes from Brighthelmston to the capital. We took this, the newest of the three available roads. Moreover, for the first stretch, it was turnpiked and the tolls therefore kept it in tolerable repair, relatively speaking. The turnpike was the 14-mile length from Brighthelmston to the Sussex village of Cuckfield. The road pushed on to Reigate in Surrey, and thence to London.

Two hazards faced the highway engineers in connecting the metropolis to the seaside town: the Downs and the Weald. The chalk hills of the North and South Downs presented problems of inclines; parts of the Weald between them presented the problem of sticky mud.

Although gaps in the South Downs were used for roads – the one we used runs through the Clayton pass – steep hills nevertheless had to be negotiated. Even at the incline at Clayton, but much more forbiddingly, the daunting rise of the hill north of the town of Reigate, could put a great strain on the horses.

The Low Weald, forming a strip across northern Sussex, is composed of the notorious Weald Clay: uninviting and infertile the year round. In rainy, cold (but not frozen) conditions, the roads become almost impenetrable: horses' hooves and vehicles' wheels are sucked into the oozing, glutinous mess; in a hot summer this metamorphoses into hard ruts of bone-jarring and teeth-rattling depth. We were travelling in early summer, but in miserably cold weather, the clouds denying the sun any chance of drying out the clay. That geological substance therefore was, at the time of our journey, persisting in its evil intent to impede the users of the roads that humans had had the impertinence to thrust over it.

What is more, the night before our journey there was heavy rainfall. Nor did it ease up during the day. Not surprisingly, when we reached the clayey area, our wheels sank. So did our hearts. More than once, Mr Pelham's coachman and manservant were forced to descend into the mud to lever, heave and push the carriage wheels out of the noxious embrace of the squelching, thick mire. And occasionally their efforts were unavailing, until I assisted. Our clothes were clotted from below by the filthy earth and soaked from above by the downpour of the water-laden sky. Mr Pelham, who was approaching 40 years of age and not sturdily built, apologised for being unable to help.

Exhausted by their efforts to extricate the carriage, the horses were too dispirited and had too few reserves of energy when we reached Reigate hill, to tackle this further obstacle with a full human load. Consequently, Mr Pelham, his servant and I had no option but to lighten the weight of the carriage by walking up that long steep geographical challenge in the rain. Although, after that effort, we were able to rest, by the time we had reached London, both Mr Pelham and I (and no doubt his servant) were tired and uncomfortable. I was unhappy and contrite; Mr Pelham was characteristically staunch in his commitment to our enterprise. While you, dear reader, will now have no doubt about our wisdom in taking bags of extra clothing with us!

We had used our time, as we travelled, to plan how we would conduct our interview with the Prince. When we arrived in London we made for a tavern in Westminster, where Mr Pelham sometimes stayed when he attended meetings of the House of Commons. We cleaned ourselves, changed our clothes and were refreshed by a substantial meal, which we consumed seated at a table close to the fire, so cold and dank was that day.

Mr Pelham recognised the urgency of our mission and suggested that we should immediately walk across St James's Park and The Mall to the Prince's London home, Carlton House. Apart from the need not to waste time, his reasons were twofold. One was to take that short walk while it was still light; the other was that we would have a greater chance of seeing the Prince at that time of the day than any other, for his late evenings and nights were often taken up with entertainments and, as a consequence, his mornings with sleeping.

Because of Mr Pelham's status as a Privy Councillor, we gained entry without any difficulty. My spirits were buoyed up, after the dreadful journey, only to be deflated: the Prince of Wales was not at Carlton House, nor even anywhere in London. He was visiting his mother, Queen Charlotte, at Windsor Castle – over 20 miles away! Another journey, though at least the road is not as treacherous as the way from Brighthelmston.

The next morning, therefore, we set forth. It was then nine days since the murder of Jonathan, and this delay – any delay – in pursuing our plans was frustrating and could potentially lead to their failure.

We arrived about noon at the impressive medieval royal castle, which so dominates the Thames and the flat Berkshire countryside.

Then more delays, as footmen questioned our business, sought out His Royal Highness in his suite of rooms, returned with a message that he would see us shortly, led us down corridors to the room where he would receive us, and – we impatiently waited.

We whiled away the slowly ticking minutes in admiring the beautifully proportioned and appointed room, with some of the newly crafted furniture of Messrs Chippendale and Sheraton.

At last, His Royal Highness arrived. My heart raced. How would he react to what we had to tell him?

I really must interpose here a little description of George, Prince of Wales, since he is such a central person in my story. He was then 33 years of age and widely admired as a handsome man, even though, to express my observations on that day delicately, from below the chest to the knees he had a decidedly portly appearance to a degree even beyond the embonpoint then so much in vogue in England. His physical attractiveness lay more in his chubby, smiling face with its slightly up-tilted end to his nose. As to his character, I had already heard that this was a confusing medley of traits. He had a fine, cultivated mind and a brilliant wit. Yet there were those, who knew him well, who described his conversation as sometimes obscene and his behaviour that of a buffoon. He was good-hearted, generous and companionable. Yet there were those with whom he associated most closely – both men and women – who were considered by his father, King George III, as scandalously unsuitable. In truth, relations between the Prince and his father were notoriously strained, in total contrast to the Prince's feelings towards his mother, and his sister Princess Elizabeth, both of whom he loved dearly, feelings that were reciprocated.

One of the causes of the tension between the King and his heir was the Prince's spendthrift mode of life: he spent money with careless lavishness on women, drinking, gambling and expensive clothes – he was indeed the King's prodigal son, though His Majesty, unlike the father in the parable recorded by St Luke, was not forgiving. In his father's eyes, the Prince was leading a life of dissipation and profligacy; in the Prince's eyes, he was being kept impoverished. When the Prince married his cousin, Princess Caroline of Brunswick (who was the daughter of the Prince's aunt Augusta) the King and Parliament agreed on the allowances the couple should receive.

The Prince had little regard politically for the Prime Minister, William Pitt, and His Royal Highness vented his spleen on that politician for what he, the Prince, considered to have been his crucial role in allocating an insufficient, penny-pinching sum.

The wedding took place on 8th April (two months before our visit). The Prince, in a state of alcoholic stupor from the effects of copious drafts of brandy, had utterly disgraced himself during the ceremony.

Such was the royal personage who now stood before us.

We bowed. The Prince welcomed the Privy Councillor affably, though, as was to be expected, with some puzzlement registering on his face. 'It is a pleasure to see you, Mr Pelham,' he said. 'But what on earth are you doing in Windsor?'

'Your Royal Highness,' Mr Pelham said, 'I apologise for intruding, but a matter of considerable import and urgency has arisen concerning your stay at Marlborough House. Moreover, because my young companion here knows so much of the detail I have presumed to ask him to attend this meeting too. May I present the Rev Benjamin Sydenham, curate of the parish of Rottingdean.'

The Prince shook my hand warmly and bade me welcome to the royal castle. 'Now, what's this all about?' he asked. 'Sounds mighty mysterious.'

Mr Pelham, as we had arranged, suggested that I simply retail the story of the murder and the uncovering of the plot so far. We had already agreed not to mention the counter-plan until the Prince had digested the basic facts.

As I told my tale, Prince George listened intently, though it was impossible for me to decipher his reaction from his face. Was he incredulous? Was he angry? Was he afraid?

'Mr Sydenham,' he said, when I had concluded, 'you have weighed your words carefully, as I would expect of an educated man, distinguishing between fact and conjecture, and explaining the reasons for your conjectures being compelling.' He turned to the Privy Councillor, and continued: 'Since you are here, Mr Pelham, and since you have brought the Rev Sydenham with you, I must assume that you believe that there is such a plot, of which he is warning me.'

Mr Pelham replied affirmatively.

'Have you, therefore, come to advise me not to come to Brighthelmston?' the Prince enquired.

'Several of us believe that the matter is not necessarily as simple as that, Your Royal Highness,' Mr Pelham replied.

'Oh!' said the Prince, his voice rising in volume. 'I would have thought there could be nothing simpler. Are you suggesting I might consider the alternative: risk the lives of myself and my wife, that is, the heir to the throne, and the Princess who is carrying my heir? Have you, a loyal and respected subject of His Majesty and a member of his Privy Council, taken leave of your senses? Or has this stripling cleric stripped them from you? Hey? Ha, ha!'

My worst fears seemed to be confirmed. I squirmed before this tirade, indirectly aimed at me. And wondered, would Mr Pelham buckle beneath this royal anger?

There followed a terrible silence. The Prince glowered. Mr Pelham – he must have expected and braced himself for such a reaction – drew a deep breath. 'Your Royal Highness,' he said, 'your response was exactly mine when I heard of this treasonous conspiracy; but I have wavered. I beg you to listen further to what we have to say. Have we your indulgence? We shall not keep you long.'

With a grunt of ill grace, the Prince invited us to continue.

As we had planned, Mr Pelham started. 'Your Royal Highness,' he said, 'if you cancel your visit, you will need to inform a number of people – your staff, your friends in London and Brighthelmston and your family, including the Princess of Wales. And you will need to cancel any arrangements – attending balls, for instance – that I am sure you will have made.'

The Prince looked concerned. He said, 'That can all be attended to of course, but it would put me in very bad repute, I own. The action would have to be explained, thus casting me as cowardly, much worse, un-gentlemanly. Am I not known as "the first gentleman in Europe"? I would be treated with contempt by Princess Caroline. She would inform her father, the Duke of Brunswick, who would spread the story through the length and breadth of the continent.'

This was much more cheering. It was now my turn to intervene. 'These are considerations of weighty importance indeed,' I said. 'But, Your Royal Highness, there is also a most cogent positive argument for keeping to your engagements. If you do not come to Brighthelmston this month, the conspirators will know that their plot has been foiled and could well engineer another scheme in the future and without the warning we now by good fortune have. Paradoxically, therefore, it would be safer for you to visit Brighthelmston as planned than not.'

The Prince allowed himself a wan smile. 'Is the Church of England appointing members of the Society of Jesus to its priesthood?' he asked. 'That's as fine a piece of Jesuitical argument I've heard for many a year!'

I was grateful for the smile: the comment was made not in chastisement but in humour, to relax the tension of the occasion.

The Prince became seriously pensive at this point. 'Now, it seems to me,' he said, after a short while, 'that if I go along with your recommendation and adhere to my arrangements, I would need assurances on two counts. One is that you can guarantee my safety and that of Princess Caroline; the second is that the desperadoes can be killed or apprehended to prevent any future attempt.'

'You have summed up the issue with admirable wisdom and conciseness, Your Royal Highness,' said Mr Pelham.

The Privy Councillor continued: 'As a matter of fact, we have devised such plans. I have taken the liberty of presenting these to His Majesty's Lord-Lieutenant in Sussex. He has written a letter to Your Royal Highness, in which, as I understand, he recommends that you hear us out before coming to a decision.

Mr Pelham handed over the letter. The Prince broke the seal, read the missive, sat down, and invited us to do so also, with a wave of the hand towards two of Mr Chippendale's fine chairs. A further silence ensued. Then, in an uncharacteristically small voice, the Prince said, 'Tell me your plans and persuade me, if you can, that they are reasonably fool-proof.'

I breathed a deep sigh of relief; I hope, inaudibly. Mr Pelham and I shared the account of the plans that had been drawn up and, by the authority of the Lord-Lieutenant, by delegation to Mr Pelham, ready to be set in motion in case the Prince would decide to go ahead with the scheme. Nor did we forget my hope that the ringleader of the planned disturbance involving the soldiery could be identified in a matter of days.

The Prince almost shouted, 'Congratulations! I consider these absolutely capital arrangements. You have made your case quite fully. What is more, even if I had doubts, I have thought of a yet more powerful argument for not abandoning my visit.'

'May we hear what that is?' asked Mr Pelham.

'Certainly,' said the Prince. 'In your account and analysis of the plot, all of you who have been collecting intelligence and planning defensive measures, have possibly overlooked, or at least underestimated, the significance of the Frenchman.'

'We have assumed, Your Royal Highness,' I said, 'that he is also a smuggler in league with the English smugglers and providing the gang with a hideout on the Normandy coast, where you and the Princess would be held until the ransom is paid.'

'That indeed is the most likely explanation. However, have you thought of other possibilities?' the Prince questioned. 'And at least one of these might suggest that the plot is even more serious than you think. The Frenchman could be in this country for any one or more of four other reasons than smuggling. He could be an *émigré*, who has settled in Brighthelmston, has exhausted what little wealth he was able to bring over with him when he fled, and is now desperate to acquire money by any means. True, that supposition does not make the plot any more serious, but it could make it easier to track him down. Or, he could be an escaped prisoner-of-war – the mental images of whom are so terrifying the people of England at the moment. However, it is difficult to see how he could exist in Brighthelmston: such an individual would scarcely find succour among the *émigrés*.

'Thank you, Your Royal Highness,' I said, 'we had not thought of these two possibilities and we shall try to investigate along these lines. But presumably if he is an escaped prisoner, he would not be any more dangerous than an *émigré*, and you have hinted that there might be greater danger than we had considered.'

'Yes indeed,' said the Prince. 'We know that there are French spies in England. This is my third category. And an escaped prisoner-of-war could have been recruited for that work. This possibility is similar to the fourth, that is, he is a secret agent sent over by the French government specially to organise my abduction. Does that not put a more serious complexion on the plot? Furthermore, if there is any likelihood that the matter is thus political, then the implications for the conduct of the war don't bear thinking about. For the motive, except for your three minor characters, would not be money, but forcing England to abandon hostilities, leaving France to dominate the continent. If there is any likelihood that this is what the plot is all about, it makes it even more imperative that I go along with your plan. Again, on this assumption, this gang must be smashed!'

The chief target of the plot emphasised this last point by bringing his fist down hard on the sturdy table next to him.

Mr Pelham was quick to follow up the Prince's last, horrendous hypothesis. 'Your last comments do, indeed, portray an appalling picture, Your Royal Highness,' he said. 'As an extra prudential measure, should we not alert the government departments responsible for spying and tracking down spies?'

'That is a first-rate idea,' said the Prince. 'Directly you have left I shall write a detailed account of our meeting and send it by fast messenger to Mr Dundas, the Secretary of State for War, to engage his crafty espionage director Evan Nepean, to see if their agents in France can uncover clues to the plot there. I know Mr Nepean well. He is a most kindly, upright and indefatigable public servant. That gives me another idea. I shall also write to the Foreign Secretary, Lord Grenville, to try to engage the help of his friend Mr Wickham, if that is possible. He knows a great deal about *émigrés* in this country through his work in the Aliens Office, though he is now organising our spying activities from Switzerland. True, I may be imaginatively exaggerating the import of this conspiracy but, I hope you agree, it is wisest to assume the worst. Whatever the motives and extent of the conspirators, as you have already acknowledged, we have no time to lose.'

We briskly agreed. I was aghast at the possible ramifications of the background to Jonathan's murder, and hence the dreadful significance of the affair in which I was now so deeply embroiled.

At another level of my consciousness, above these silent musings, I was aware that the Prince was talking to me. He was saying: 'You and your friends, Mr Sydenham, must resume your investigations. Also, please give my kindest regards to the poor, ailing Mr Hamilton and tell him that I look forward to seeing him anon. Of course, it goes without saying that I shall be forever in your debt. Do please call upon me in Marlborough House: I shall send you an invitation.'

I thanked him most sincerely. Then we took our leave.

Fortunately, the journey back to Brighthelmston was rather less trying than our earlier gruesome experience. When I arrived home I was welcomed rapturously by Billy with the loudest vibrations of purring I had ever heard, and with serpentine movements round my legs to rub his head and ears, thus unintentionally impeding my progress into the cottage. I later reported to Thomas Hooker our success in recruiting the

66

Prince of Wales to our scheme and the awful possible true motive for the plot. Unfortunately, he had no information of his own.

The next day James and Mary did have an item of news to tell me – of little import we reckoned at the time, though of cardinal importance, as it turned out. James explained that, two days before, they had received a visit from the constable. He had come to report that he had gone to the Greenway coastguard station and cottages to interview the men there. His reasoning was as follows. I had seen Jonathan's assailant galloping in the direction of these buildings and the constable wondered if anyone else had seen him. According to James, he proudly explained that he gave all the details I had reported to him to the Greenway inhabitants to help jog their memories. Though, unfortunately, this was to no avail: no one had seen any strangers that evening. He just wanted to impress upon the bereaved that he was still working on the crime.

James made the obvious comment that the constable did not seem to be making much headway. He then smiled and, changing the subject, said, 'Mary and I wondered if you would care to come with us to have supper with Jane Patcham at her uncle and aunt's house tomorrow evening? We are certain that you would find them interesting people and they are very eager to meet you.'

I blurted out a rapid, 'Oh, yes, please, and thank you very much.' Another opportunity to be close to Mary.

James and I returned to our serious discussion. We calculated that the soldier we wished to identify would be released from his confinement that evening, and that we should therefore go to 'The George' in the expectation that he would be there, making up for lost drinking time over the past week.

I spent the rest of the day in Rottingdean, mostly attending to the social and nutritional needs of my feline pet, my equine mount and parochial flock. Late in the afternoon Dr Hooker came looking for me, and found me in the church checking the vestments. He was in a highly excited state.

'It's to be Monday 17th June,' he said, in a confidential whisper.

'What is "it"?' I asked.

'The kidnapping,' he said.

I was stunned at the suddenness of the information he had to give me, and its precision, pleased that we were now accurately forewarned, and still had a fair number of days in hand to make our preparations.

'How did you come by this intelligence?' I asked in response.

'Talking to one of my fisherman friends a little while ago. Someone who dabbles in the other activities of which I have spoken,' the vicar said with a naughty smile. 'My acquaintance has been recruited for what we know fairly clearly is the diversionary landing of goods here. He, of course, is not privy to this purpose, and is exceedingly perplexed as to why such a precise date, so many days away, has been specified. That's why he mentioned it to me. Naturally, I told him I was equally puzzled. I am sure that I can be forgiven that falsehood.'

Despite not being his confessor, I said I absolved him and gave him my heartiest and heartfelt congratulations.

That evening, when James and I entered 'The George', there were several knots of soldiers already there. We were later than we had intended because James, Mary and I had spent some time discussing Thomas's discovery. We bought our drinks and wandered around inspecting all those in uniform, but trying desperately to pretend that we were intent on our gossip and beverage.

James was worried. When he had seen the conspirators the week before, he had caught only a glimpse; and in the interim his memory of the private's face had faded somewhat. Furthermore, there were two soldiers present that evening who seemed to match the one he had originally observed. He indicated these to me. Throughout the evening I looked at these faces with as much seeming casualness as possible, and from different angles, in order to imprint them on my memory.

For we had not the advantage of either of these men being in conversation with any of the other conspirators as had happened when James had made his initial sighting.

The next day I was going to be excessively busy. To Messrs Hamilton and Pelham to report Dr Hooker's crucial information; to the army camp to describe our two suspects to the commanding officer; and with the Prestons to go on to meet the Patcham family in the evening. I was not leading a dull life at that time; that was certain!

Chapter 7

This busy day was Friday, 7th June, ten days before the planned
abduction of the Prince and Princess of Wales. My priority
that morning was to visit Mr Pelham in Stanmer. My route
took me almost due north over the farmland of the Downs to
the village of Falmer, where I met the road from Brighthelmston
to Lewes. Stanmer lies but a short distance from there. The
weather was overcast and cool, though not raining. I was
glad to be wearing my thick coat.

Mr Pelham greeted me genially. We sat down, and he
explained that he was working on papers relating to his recent
appointment as Chief Secretary to the Lord-Lieutenant of
Ireland, prior to visiting Dublin Castle. I came quickly to the
reason for my calling, namely, Dr Hooker's discovery of the
date fixed by the conspirators for activating their plan.

'This is extremely valuable information,' he said. 'I must
organise the introduction of the guards into Marlborough House
to accord with this date. We don't want them there for too
long, kicking their heels, becoming bored. Also, the longer
they are there before the assault, the more their presence may
be discovered and your ruse brought to naught.'

'How will the troops forming the guard be selected?' I
asked.

'I was just about to tell you,' he said, 'that, following discreet
enquiries, I have discovered that the soldiers in the new infantry
barracks behind 'The King and Queen' inn are highly reliable

and hence most suitable for the role. Also, I have seen the Barrack Master and made the arrangements.'

'Very appropriately near,' I said.

'That gives me another thought,' said the Deputy Lieutenant. 'I will now write a note to that commanding officer, which I would be most obliged if you would take, informing him of the date. Would that inconvenience you too much?'

'By no means, sir,' I said. 'My arrangement is to go from here to see the commanding officer of the camp. I can stop at the barracks on the way.'

'Splendid!' said Mr Pelham. He rapidly wrote the note and handed it to me, saying, 'So let us now about our errands.'

We shook hands as if friends, and I left, content that our plan was under way in such a satisfactory manner. Ten minutes or so later I presented myself to the Barrack Master, who, when he read the note, explained that, as a consequence of Mr Pelham's visit, he had already ear-marked the soldiers he would detail for this supremely important and delicate task.

'I shudder to think what my fate would be if my men failed in this operation,' he said, 'so I'm deeply grateful for any intelligence I can be given. Thank you, and please thank Dr Hooker.'

I told him that I was now off to visit the camp. He looked slightly baffled and worried.

'Forgive me,' I said. 'I'm not about to complicate your task,' and started to outline the matter of identifying the ringleader of the related action there; but the commander of the barracks had already been told by the camp commander.

The colonel who was to command the full camp had arrived in response to the captain's message. He greeted me warmly. He was a man of mature years, starting to grey, though gave every appearance of mental and physical fitness for his task. I discovered, as we talked, that he was a soldier of considerable experience in the wars England had fought in recent decades, and had been fully briefed by the captain about the plot, as I had understood it, the week before. For my part, I now had a great deal extra to report: the involvement of the Lord-Lieutenant and the Deputy Lieutenant and, most importantly, our visit to Windsor. I then went on to the observations made by James and myself in 'The George', following the recommendation of the captain, now the colonel's adjutant. The colonel summoned him to join us. He listened to my descriptions of the two privates who matched James's initial sighting of the soldier with the other conspirators.

Unfortunately, so vague were my details, that the adjutant thought our conspirator could be any of several privates about whom he had particular suspicions. The problem was, how to identify the correct man. The captain's favoured candidate was one Silas Smith, a surly individual who had already been put on a charge for insolence to a corporal, and was one of those soldiers who had been confined to camp because of the disturbance at the inn. We had the problems now of making sure he was our man and discovering what he was planning.

The adjutant came up with an idea. He addressed his commanding officer. 'Sir,' he said, 'could I make a suggestion?'

'By all means,' said the colonel.

'The number of men in camp is already too large for the Rev Sydenham and his friend to identify our suspects at a full morning parade, for example, and it would arouse suspicion if they attended, in any case. We therefore need an excuse to assemble a small selection of the camp – including, of course, the suspects – in the presence of Mr Sydenham and Mr Preston in circumstances that would appear natural.'

'I understand the basic idea,' the colonel said, 'but how the devil – I beg your pardon, Mr Sydenham – can we possibly devise such a gathering?'

The adjutant continued: 'My proposal is that we be bold; that we respond both to the current unease in the town about the court martial and to the demands for many more men to have the vote, that are being made by the political Radicals in the country at large – even promoted in the House of Lords by the Duke of Richmond, the Lord-Lieutenant of this county.

That is, we convene a meeting of our selection of troops together with representatives of the local community, invite our men to air any grievances they have and for you, sir, to respond, explaining what is and what is not practicable. By holding such a meeting, both the soldiers and the civilians would understand the problems. But the real purpose would be the identification of the soldier-conspirator. I would arrange to be among the civilians, and 'happen' to be next to Mr Sydenham and Mr Preston, who can point out who they think might be their man.'

'That is extraordinarily ingenious,' the commanding officer said. 'But, as you hinted, also somewhat perilous. I shall need to think about this, and work through the details. For example, you did not mention the units in the infantry and cavalry barracks. As I understand it, our bad chap is planning trouble there and, in any case, if the expressed purpose of the assembly is for soldiers and civilians to exchange views, we cannot restrict the representatives of the soldiery just to the camp. I have already informed the commanding officers of the two barracks, by the way, about this problem – particularly delicate for the infantry colonel, who, I understand, is supplying the secret bodyguard. Would it be convenient for the three of us to meet again on Sunday afternoon?'

I assented both to the scheme and the extra meeting, and added that I would explain the scheme to Mr Preston, who, I was certain, would also endorse these arrangements.

'By the way,' said the captain, as an afterthought, 'Private Smith sports a useful aid to recognition, which might not have been noticeable in the crush of men in the inn: he is heavily built with – er – an obvious frontal protuberance.'

We all appreciated the humour, and the thought passed through my mind that Dr Hooker was not the only one who can produce an instantaneous and apt euphemism.

I took my leave, and then made my way, via James's shop, to tell Mr Hamilton about Dr Hooker's discovery of the date. The door was opened, as usual, by Henry the manservant, who, it seemed, was not all that pleased to see me. I assumed this was because Mr Hamilton was not feeling very well, as Henry told me. He none the less announced me.

I explained that we now had a precise date, and that the soldiers to act as bodyguards had already been picked.

'I am glad that matters are all now going to plan,' he said. 'Although I must confess that as the details are falling into place, I am becoming somewhat nervous. Do you know the poetry of the Scotsman, the young Mr Burns?' he asked.

I admitted that I did not, and was baffled by the question.

'So you have not read his 'To a Mouse',' the MP said with a touch of sadness in his voice.

I repeated my admission. I had come to convey to Mr Hamilton vital information about a forthcoming event that could put the country in great hazard, and he was talking about a Scottish poem dedicated to a rodent!

He then recited: 'The best laid schemes o' mice an' men Gang aft a-gley'.

It was hardly to be wondered at that the Scotsman's thought did not boost my confidence. (I assumed that 'a-gley' means 'awry'.)

It was Mr Hamilton's turn to give me information. By-the bye,' he said, in a manner suggesting an unimportant casual afterthought, 'Their Royal Highnesses will be arriving tomorrow.'

That was Saturday, 8th June. In the discussions I had had with Mr Hamilton and the Prince, neither of them had divulged the precise date. As it happened, we still had nine days before the planned kidnap.

'Ah,' Mr Hamilton continued, 'and in his note, that the messenger delivered just before you arrived, the Prince has asked that you should visit us tomorrow evening.' Typical of a Prince, I thought, that he should expect everyone to meet his requests at short notice; and of the casual, and admittedly ailing, Mr Hamilton, not to have alerted the key authorities.

I gave my thanks, left, and hurried to report again to the commanding officer of the infantry barracks and Mr Pelham. In fact, as the Barrack Master now told me, the Lord-Lieutenant had already informed him of the date.

I felt both relieved to learn of this efficiency, but at the same time, again upset that no one had thought to let me know. This was not an affront to my pride, for I pride myself in suffering little of that vice! Furthermore, I calmed my irritation by telling myself that I was only a curate, totally outside the military and security services that were handling the planning. However, when I called on Mr Pelham, I discovered that he had not been told. My relief that the system was working properly was dissipated. The Prince had communicated with the Lord-Lieutenant, who had communicated with the commander of the barracks, by-passing his Deputy Lieutenant, to whom he had delegated this task, and who had dutifully kept him informed of the progress of our plans. Perhaps this was typical and I should not have been surprised!

That evening, I brushed my clothes and excitedly waited for the time to ride to the Prestons' home and then to proceed with them to the Patchams.

Mr George Patcham and Mrs Charlotte Patcham owned a small shop in The Steyne, where, helped by their daughter Henrietta, they sold an amazing medley of goods – toys, ribbons, china, lace, cotton and linen underwear, all incredibly densely displayed. They lived a little distance away in one of the new houses in Church Street, an area just being built upon to the north of the old town.

The Patchams were, indeed, as Mary had told me, a charming family. After the meal, Henrietta and her father entertained us, she singing in a small but sweet voice, accompanied by Mr Patcham playing the flute. We all avoided the subject of Jonathan in our conversation, as being too painful for Jane.

As James, Mary and I walked back to the Preston home we met Tom Hudson returning from the church to his vicarage.

I stayed to explain where we had been, while Mary and James walked on, no doubt not knowing how long we two clerics would gossip. Then, as they rounded a corner in the maze of small lanes, twittens and courts, a man wielding a knife, jumped out from a doorway.

Mary shouted, 'look out!' – a shout I could not fail to hear. I ran towards her cry faster than I thought my legs could carry me, propelled by my dreadful fear. The man, who was lunging at James, was momentarily startled, a hesitation that slightly deflected his aim. The knife sliced deeply into the shoulder of Mary's cloak. Maddened by the sight of Mary's blood staining the cloth, I threw the whole of my, admittedly slight, weight on to the man. I grabbed the assailant's wrist with both hands, simultaneously twisting it swiftly and viciously with all my strength. The force and unexpectedness of my counter-attack pushed our enemy against a shop window. I pulled his wrist towards me and then immediately slammed it against the corner window-frame. His grip on the knife, already weakened by my twisting motion to the wrist, slackened completely. The knife, slicked with blood, dropped to the ground.

By now, my friend Tom had come running up. A pity, but we could not hold the attacker. He recovered from the impetus of my assault, pushed me away with considerable force, wrenching his wrist from my hands and ran off at great speed. While James was tending his daughter, Tom and I gave chase, but lost him in the confused labyrinth. However, I had noticed, in our brief struggle, that he displayed a dark multi-coloured bruise on one of his cheeks.

Mary left her distracted father, stepped over to me and collapsed into my arms, thanking me for rescuing them. Tom raced off to North Street to fetch Dr Henderson, the physician; I escorted the shocked James and the wounded and frightened Mary to their home.

James helped Mary to remove her cloak and tore away the portion of her dress to expose the cut, while I busied myself in the kitchen filling bowls of water and collecting a towel. James took the towel to put on his daughter's wounded shoulder to staunch the flow of blood. Very soon, Dr Henderson and Tom arrived, both breathless. The physician pronounced the cut shoulder not at all dangerous and applied a salve and dressing. What a blessing that the weather was so cold that Mary was therefore wearing a thick cloak with its hood lowered to her shoulders, which stopped the knife from biting too far into the flesh.

Tom and the physician left. James and Mary asked me to stay.

James dispensed generous measures of brandy, which helped us all to relax and recover. Mary said she wanted to talk about the attack; I said she should rest and that we should talk the next day; she insisted; I surrendered!

'It is obvious,' she said, 'that this evening's attack is connected with Jonathan's murder and the plot against the Prince of Wales. The man with the knife was the man father saw in 'The George', because of the bruise on his cheek.' I had mentioned this as we walked away from the scene of the assault: since the man attacked from behind and both James and Mary were terrified, they had not seen their assailant's face. 'So,' she continued, 'he must have seen father watching him in the inn and decided that this observation might foretell danger. He intended to kill father, or at least wound and frighten him sufficiently to deter him from any further visits to 'The George'. I must have stepped in the way, and you, Ben, courageously disarmed him.'

I was uncomfortably aware of my cheeks reddening.

'I feel so responsible,' I said. 'I should have allowed the constable to undertake the enquiries. I've made you, James, the target for another murderous attack and you, dearest Mary, an injured victim.'

'Nonsense,' said James. 'We would not have wished to leave the matter to that man, too busy to deal with this intricate and dangerous case beyond his experience, would we, Mary?'

'Certainly not,' she declared, with considerable firmness. 'And don't you dare feel any guilt for one second, Ben.'

James then said, 'your mention of the constable reminds me: you remember we told you about his visit to us?'

'Yes,' I said.

'Well,' James continued, 'to lighten the atmosphere, as he thought, the constable added, with a grin, that one of the coastguards, Ned North, had obviously been in a fight because he had a large bruise on his cheek.'

'That confirms the reason for this evening's incident,' I said. 'Mr North probably realised the constable would report to you and that would have made him doubly frightened. But the constable's, albeit innocent, blundering has benefited us because we can now put a name to that rascal. Also, I've just thought: could you not ask the constable to search his cottage for Jonathan's watch and prints?'

'That's a first-rate idea,' Mary said. 'And it is good that we probably have two names out of four, if we can confirm Silas Smith at the special assembly.'

'But who is the third English conspirator, the smuggler?' I wondered aloud. 'Remember, he was not in 'The George' when the Frenchman met the soldier and the coastguard. And I asked Dr Hooker to make enquiries, yet so far he has come up with nothing. I must see him tomorrow, to let him know the latest turn of events and press him to try to track down our elusive smuggler.'

'I think I might have an explanation for his elusiveness,' Mary said. 'The plan comprises two operations, one in Brighthelmston and the other in Rottingdean. It is likely that the smuggler has been given the task of organising the Rottingdean diversion only, so he would not have been required at the discussions in 'The George' about the main activities in the town here.'

'All the more reason,' I said, 'for stressing to Thomas how much we are relying on him to find out the name of the smuggler. At the same time, we must not forget the Frenchman, either. When I see the Prince tomorrow evening I will ask if he has heard anything from the espionage and security services; though, in all conscience, it is early days yet.'

'I will try to make casual enquiries of my French customers,' James said. 'It comes to my mind as well that we haven't recently been in touch with Mrs Gunn, the recipient of all local gossip. Perhaps we should ask her if she has heard of the recent arrival of a Frenchman.'

'That's a good suggestion,' I said. 'I'll do that tomorrow. While I'm talking to her I can ask if she has any special message I can take for her to her friend the Prince of Wales!'

This comment produced a chuckle. Then James became serious.

'After Mr North's attempt this evening, we must be careful not to endanger other people's lives,' he said. 'Any one of these desperadoes who believed someone had an inkling of what they are up to, or even just being able to name Jonathan's murderer, could be in danger of another attempted killing.'

'I will make my meeting with the dipper look quite casual,' I said.

'But don't forget yourself,' said James. 'Especially after your tussle this evening, you are as much at risk as Mary and me. I have a sword-stick, which I shall now always carry. A friend of my father gave it to me as a present and coached me in its efficient use. You should have one too.'

This advice shocked me. 'I am a man of the cloth,' I said. 'I cannot go about armed with a lethal weapon. A cane, yes, to defend myself, but if I used the blade of a sword-stick, I could kill anyone who assailed me. I would never live in peace if that happened.'

'I can indeed understand that,' said Mary, 'yet I beg you to give more thought to father's suggestion. I have already lost a brother; I could not bear to lose my dearest friend as well.'

James added: 'An unsheathed blade of a sword-stick can be a powerful deterrent to any attacker, and can be used to disarm by injuring a hand or arm without inflicting a mortal wound. Mr Williams, the tailor in East Street who sells gentlemen's accessories, stocks these items. Sleep on the idea, Ben; and I hope that when you come to see Martha Gunn tomorrow you will call into that shop too.'

I agreed to consider the proposal that I should arm myself. I left at last. The picture I could not remove from my mind's eye as Betsy conveyed me home was of Mary's pleading eyes as she bade me good night.

Chapter 8

There is no difficulty in finding a vicar on a Saturday. He will be in his study writing his sermon for the following day. I interrupted Thomas Hooker's furrowed brow and flowing pen. It mattered little: he had a full and fertile mind and translated his consequent wisdom with ease into telling and fluent messages to his congregation.

'Haven't seen you for a little while, Ben,' he said. 'Have you been idle?' he teased.

Ignoring the jest, except for a weak smile, I continued my narrative from the point where I had left it at our last meeting, causing him to look grimly worried. I then got to the tricky point: 'I have two favours to ask you, Thomas.'

He grinned, and said, '*Quid pro quo*, eh? You entertain me with your exploits and I, in return, salve your conscience. Is that it?'

I felt awkward. 'Well,' I explained, 'One matter is an issue of conscience.' I put the question bluntly, blurting it out in my embarrassment: 'Should I buy a sword-stick?'

'Are you asking me as a theologian or as a friend?' he asked.

'Both,' I replied.

'My answer, as a friend, is an unequivocal "yes". You and your companions in this affair are in obvious danger and you must have some effective means of defence for yourself and to assist their defence should the occasion arise again. You were lucky to have worsted the assailant last evening. My answer as a theologian is more difficult. It is said that, in the eleventh century, Odo, Bishop of Bayeux, enjoyed fighting in battles but used as his weapon a mace, not a sword or battle-axe, so as to bludgeon his enemies and avoid spilling their blood, because that was forbidden of a cleric.'

'Do you, then, leave me to decide?' I asked, with some perturbation of my soul.

'I will assist you, my son,' the vicar said in his characteristically helpful way. 'I would commend a compromise prudently planned. Your friend Mr Preston knows how to use the weapon. You buy one, as he has urged you to, and take lessons from him in how to handle it, so that, in the event of an encounter, you can inflict the minimum of wounding on your adversary.'

I thanked him – by no means for the first time for his wise counsel. I then asked him for the second favour.

'The other piece of help is, I'm sorry to say, more difficult for you to give,' I said. 'As I have explained, we now have the identity of the coastguard-conspirator, are on the verge of identifying the soldier- conspirator and are now concentrating on putting a name to the Frenchman. The smuggler in the plot has not been knowingly seen, since Jonathan spied his back-view after he overheard the conspirators' conversation. Since the smuggler is involved in the Rottingdean operation, I wonder if you could help me in finding him.'

'Yes,' said Thomas, 'you've asked for my help on this matter before. I've been even more alert than usual to gossip among the fishermen and agricultural workers who have a tendency to engage in this secondary employment....'

Another felicitous euphemism!

'But I've gathered nothing.'

'In some ways,' I admitted, 'he is the least important of the quartet. Their plan of drawing attention to Rottingdean and so lower alertness at Brighthelmston won't work because we know the whole scheme. On the other hand, we mustn't forget our other objective, namely, bringing Jonathan's murderer to justice.'

'But how could identifying this man help in that endeavour?' Thomas asked. 'From what you have told me, it looks fairly obvious that Mr North committed that appalling crime.'

'Yes, true,' I said; 'the few hints that we have lead to him. However, there are two reasons in connection with the murder for wanting to track down the smuggler. One is that we must have proof in order to convict Ned North, and the smuggler might be willing to inform on his co-conspirator for fear, otherwise, of being himself arrested as an accessory to the crime. The second reason is simpler: the smuggler himself might be the murderer. We can't be absolutely certain that it was Mr North.'

'I see,' said the vicar. 'They are both compelling arguments. Yet what more can we do? Have you any ideas?'

'As you can imagine,' I said, 'I have been giving a fair amount of thought to the problem. The results of all this mental effort run along the following lines. The Rottingdean smugglers are not hardened criminals, nor would they take the risk of being implicated in an act of treason, as this plot assuredly is. Our man must therefore be of a different stamp from the others or desperate, from excessive greed or dire necessity, for extra money. Moreover, however determined he is, he will be nervous, and increasingly so as 17th June draws nearer.'

Thomas pondered a while. Then, with a cunning smile, he said, 'I have just had a thought; I think it might work. I will write a different sermon for tomorrow and I want you to watch the congregation carefully to see if any man is particularly discomfited by what I say.'

This sounded very mysterious, though it was evident that I would have to wait until the next morning to discover the trap the vicar was going to lay from the pulpit.

I rode straight off to Brighthelmston to engage in some shopping. I needed to buy a new pair of shoes from Mr Dine's shop in Market Street. I was unused to attending smart dinner parties and my only footwear were disreputably worn. It had suddenly come to me in the middle of the night that the Prince of Wales, a stickler for smart fashion, would consider me disrespectful if I wore even the better of my two pairs of shoes at his dinner party.

My other purchase, which I made at Mr Williams's shop, with considerable nervousness and uncertainty, was a sword-stick. I had not realised that there were two kinds. One, where the stick is in effect a scabbard, and to use the sword one has to un-sheath it. The other, newfangled version contains a spring connected to a dagger inside the end of the hollow stick; by releasing the spring with a trigger in the handle, the blade shoots out. It was quite obvious that the second kind would be more suitable for me. The first type commits the owner to using either stick or blade; the second type allows the owner to delay exposing the blade until the use of the stick to ward off the attacker proves unavailing.

I took my purchases to the Prestons' home. Mary much admired my shoes; James much admired my sword-stick; and both admired my resolve in buying the latter. I recounted my conversation with Dr Hooker about the weapon, which in my heart I thought I could never bring myself to use except as a cudgel.

James willingly agreed to give me some practice. Leaving Mary in the shop, we went into the parlour and rearranged the furniture in order to give ourselves some space for mock encounters. Using his sword-stick (sheathed!) and a ruler to simulate a knife, dagger or pistol, James showed me how to parry, thrust and feint and to disarm an assailant. I felt awkward and self-conscious at first. James urged me on, becoming increasingly aggressive, forcing me to react, and correcting my false moves. After nearly an hour he judged me reasonably competent, declaring with a titter that he would feel safe if I accompanied him even in the most forbidding, murky and dangerous parts of London!

When my lesson had obviously ended – no more laboured breathing! – Mary came to enquire how proficient the pupil had proved to be. James was duly complimentary (or kind).

Having helped to restore the parlour to its normal tidiness, rested a little and taken some light refreshment, I made my way to the beach to find Martha Gunn. She greeted me jovially; I gave her the newest information, notably the assault the previous evening, and she commended me on my defensive acquisition. I then broached the subject of the Frenchman, recalling my conversation on that subject with the Prince.

'Most of the Frenchies here,' she said, 'are supporters of the old regime and they've suffered at the hands of the bloodthirsty revolutionaries. They wouldn't help an escaped prisoner-of-war. And what do you think they'd do to a spy!'

'But suppose a secret agent of the Committee of Public Safety came to Brighthelmston, posing, with a false identity, as someone who had been a victim of the French government's policies. He would be befriended, surely?' I suggested.

Martha agreed. 'I see,' she said. 'You want me to try and find out if there have been any new arrivals and what sort they are. It shouldn't be too hard. There haven't been all that many since little weaselly Robespierre had his head chopped off a year ago.'

I thanked the dipper. Then I collected Betsy from where I had tethered her, and rode back to Rottingdean. I spent some time that afternoon grooming her – a form of attention she much enjoyed, and which was observed by Billy, who always decided that this was a cue for his self-grooming. Betsy, Billy and I were great friends, and there was no jealousy between horse and cat. They were both advanced in years and I dreaded the days, not long ahead, when they would no longer be with me.

Thomas had kindly given me Betsy as a welcoming present when I became his curate; she was too old for his needs by then and he was glad to know that she would be useful to someone who would constantly care for her. As to Billy, he just walked into the cottage after I had been living there for about a month, decided that this would be his home and that he could ensure I would behave properly towards him. He did not seem to object to the name I conferred upon him. Nor, I am pleased to say, did Mrs Heath object to the extra lodger.

While thus engaged with Betsy, I tried to picture our own male parishioners, wondering who might be the smuggler-conspirator. If he was someone in need of money, that could include so many of our poverty-stricken villagers during these dreadfully harsh times. How was I to narrow down the suspects? There could be three possible reasons for a man to be driven to desperation for income beyond what he himself could provide for his family, supplemented by the parish. One was having an extra large number of children; another was an addiction to alcohol; and a third was another addiction, namely, gambling.

This quiet thinking proved beneficial to my slow brain: of course I knew which families had large numbers of children and whose fathers earned very little. They were the families I visited most regularly with my alms of bread and cheese. I still had time to call on them all before going to Marlborough House. I reckoned that five families still fitted that description after the bitter winter: four others had lost several little ones and in the case of one other, the father had died at that time. Of the five fathers whose families I was therefore now going to see, three worked on the land and two were fishermen.

I collected the food, walked to the cottages and was, as always, welcomed with tears of gratitude by the mothers of the poor, thin wretches of children. I chatted, hoping to discover something about their men's habits, but without gathering anything useful. On the other hand, in one cottage I saw a set of dominoes and, in another, a draughtboard. Perfectly innocent in themselves – they could have been used to pass the long winter evenings that farm labourers had to endure, or in times of storm when fishermen could not put to sea. Still – they might have been indications of gambling.

Patient readers, I fear that I must interrupt my narrative again. There may be those among you who might think that we would not have considered a farm-worker as our smuggler-conspirator, that he must have been a fisherman. But that was not necessarily so. The contraband goods were brought across the English Channel by organised gangs; what was required of the Rottingdean men was to unload the casks and boxes and transport them inland for distribution. Strong farm-workers, used to handling horses and heavy loads of hay and sheaves of wheat, were ideal for this work, as much as, if not more than the fishermen, who, with their knowledge of tides, and habits of making their catches at night, provided that different expert assistance.

I must pass now swiftly to the grand social event at Marlborough House that evening.

Fortunately, the weather was dry after the torrential downpour of the day before, when the Prince and Princess arrived in Brighthelmston. The people, who had congregated to welcome the royal couple, were drenched and the rain ruined the arranged firework display, though the Prince graciously walked around in the rain to acknowledge the welcome that had been intended. When we arrived for the dinner, not surprisingly, the weather was the immediate topic of conversation. In terms of the numbers of guests, compared with the Prince's usual expansive entertainment, it was an exceedingly modest affair. After all, the royal party had only just arrived, and the cloud of the abduction plot, albeit some days away, including the arrangements for their protection now in hand, must have tempered the Prince's exuberance. We were just six: the Prince, the Princess, Mr Hamilton, Mr and Mrs Pelham and myself.

Mr Hamilton had never married, and Marlborough House seemed very large for a bachelor. I had not realised how spacious it was until that evening. Henry, the manservant, led me from the richly decorated hall into a magnificent drawing room, the elegance of which was enhanced by the fine fireplace, wrought, as Mr Hamilton told me, of Sicilian marble. There, the Prince, Princess and Mr Hamilton were seated, conversing and drinking. I executed low bows to Their Royal

Highnesses and a shallow one to Mr Hamilton. The Prince welcomed me and introduced me to his wife, who said that she was very pleased to meet me, speaking with a thick German accent. Mr Hamilton then stood up and shook my hand – I noticed that, though ailing, he was still a tall, elegant man, features I had not appreciated when he was seated nor when we had previously met. This observation reminded me of something Tom Hudson had told me: this was a description of Mr Hamilton by the famous writer, Fanny Burney, of his being 'extremely tall and handsome; has an air of haughty and fashionable superiority; is intelligent, dry, sarcastic and clever.' She apparently added 'crafty' for good measure!

Mr and Mrs Pelham arrived shortly. Then, after desultory conversation, Henry entered to announce that dinner was served.

The dining room, octagonal in shape and with a domed ceiling, is even more worthy of admiration than the drawing room. Although we were small in number, a sizeable table was set in the middle of the room. In the centre there arose a superb arrangement, known, as I learned later, by the French term '*surtout de table*'. The dominant feature was a collection of figurines representing goddesses and cherubs holding garlands. Surrounding these were miniature trees and hedges; and to add to the glory of the display, small dishes spread out containing pyramids of fruit decorated with leaves.

Space was also needed at each placement for mighty arrays of cutlery and glasses, for the sumptuous meal of which we were to partake. Furthermore, each diner was attended by a server, supervised by Henry, who clearly possessed a practised and disciplining eye. When we were all seated, His Royal Highness declared that he was truly delighted to see us and hoped that we would enjoy our meal despite the fact that it was so frugal – due to the shortage of time for its preparation. Only twenty-five items were on the menu and merely a dozen choices of wine! The Prince then asked me to say grace.

I started my meal, the like of which I had never seen, let

alone tasted before, with *garbure aux choux*, a thick creamy soup flavoured with cabbage. I followed this with trout cooked in oil with garlic and tomatoes. Then a little braised goose; then lamb cutlets; then a finely moulded orange glacée; then a praline gâteau. Then ... but I could eat no more, even though the meal took four hours, the food washed down with fine wines, and the gourmand Prince urged me at intervals in disappointed tones to taste other offerings, which he assured me – and I believed him – were delicious. I explained that, as an indigent curate, my stomach was not attuned to repasts of such rich variety, and begged to be excused.

As the wine flowed freely, so conversation rippled with mounting vigour round the table. I soon learned that the Princess enjoyed joking, though was sadly lacking in tact as she gossiped about her husband and his dissolute friends.

However, the highlight of the evening, in human terms, was the delightful way the Prince behaved: charming to all, exchanging witty banter with Mr Hamilton and, above all, mimicking famous people to hilarious effect. At times we were all helpless with laughter. My favourite, I remember to this day, was the Prince's William Pitt. I have already reported how much His Royal Highness disliked the Prime Minister. And what was incredible about that evening's performance – I can think of no more apt word – was that the heir to the throne seemed to reshape his fleshy visage to look like the pinched-faced, pointed-nosed statesman who was unsparingly to lead Britain for many more years in the titanic conflict with France.

As I recorded in my diary the next day, the entertainment proceeded as follows.

The Prince rose from his chair and addressed us. 'Has there ever been such a pompous political leader of this country as Mr Pitt? A fortnight ago, as my good friend Charles James Fox told me, the Prime Minister made one of his tedious speeches in the House of Commons. He was replying to the motion by Mr Wilberforce – friend of Mr Pitt's, by-the-bye –

for England to follow other countries in arranging to cease hostilities with France. I give you a few extracts.'

The Prince reorganised his face and stance for his quotations from the speech, by no means all of which, I confess, I could remember to record. Therefore, just an indication of the entertainment I note down here. He started with the Prime Minister addressing the Speaker of the House of Commons thus:

"'I shall certainly endeavour, Sir, to confine what I have to say to the real point under discussion." Yet only after a great accumulation of sentences did he get to the point. Then on and on, with interpolations: "But another question here arises"! … "The next argument is". Ah! But he did eventually change his approach, no doubt to make the speech more interesting, to "In the next place"! Oh, even so, ladies and gentlemen, we must be fair, because at the end of this "succinct" speech, Mr Pitt did have the decency to admit: "I have trespassed too long on the patience of this house". So, he was coming at last to his conclusion. Yet, not before uttering this gem about Parliament's responsibility for Britain's condition: "You have laid on taxes unprecedented in their amount, but at the same time having the satisfaction you know that they are borne by the inhabitants of this country without material pressure."'

During this recital the Prince modulated his voice and changed his expression, carrying us along with his own incredulity that the Prime Minister got *rapidly* to his point, producing from us, his audience, great gusts of laughter. Then, following the last quotation, he changed his mood, commenting, 'Is our Prime Minister so utterly ignorant of the level of smuggling to evade the punitive customs and excise duties, and – so much more serious a lack of comprehension – of the parlous state of the country's poor?' We fell into an appropriate silence.

Thus, with impressive skill, did His Royal Highness, like a talented actor, carry us through elements of comedy and tragedy.

Maybe it was deliberate, but the Prince gave this theatrical rendering after we had finished our meal. He then said, 'Ladies and gentlemen, the questions of our relationship with France and of smuggling, I am sure, must remind us of the forthcoming threat to Her Royal Highness and myself. Forgive me for raising this serious matter at the end of such a delightful evening; however, I would be deeply grateful if the ladies would retire to the drawing room, where, I am sure, they will have topics of mutual interest to talk about. Meanwhile, gentlemen, I would be indebted to you if we could discuss for a while, over our port, brandy and tobacco, arrangements for 17th June.'

This we did, including a contribution from me concerning our most up-to-date information about the conspirators and plans to gain more. I mentioned our lack of detail about the Frenchman. The Prince replied, after a moment's thought, that he would dispatch a message to Mr Dundas asking him to send Mr Nepean to come to see me. Then Mr Hamilton took us on a tour of the house to show us where the bodyguards would be accommodated and where the Prince and Princess would be secreted on the night of the attack.

I slept very little during the small amount of the night that was left when I arrived home. The evening had been such an exciting and enjoyable experience; nor was it easy to command sleep when my stomach was uncomfortably full. There was yet another factor inhibiting somnolence: Sunday was to be busy and interesting. There was the mystery of Dr Hooker's sermon to trap the smuggler, and the chance of identifying the soldier.

Chapter 9

I knew that I had dropped off to sleep eventually, because I was woken by a combination of Billy's purring and nuzzling by my left ear and the sound of the church bell summoning worshippers penetrating the cottage walls. I then became aware of Mrs Heath's rhythmical hammering on my door with her fist and shouting my name. I had unforgivably overslept that Sunday morning. No time for breakfast, though no doubt Mrs Heath took pity on Billy for my neglect of his needs. I shouted thanks to her through the door, washed my face, shaved and dressed at great speed and raced across to the church.

As usual, the congregation nearly filled the pews. Apart from their faith, the villagers liked Thomas as a kindly person and interesting preacher. I positioned myself the best I could, as he had instructed, so as to observe any reactions to the sermon he had especially written for that Sunday morning.

When that part of the service came, he walked up the steps into the pulpit and addressed his parishioners in his clear voice:

'The lesson this morning is taken from the Gospel according to St Matthew, Book XXVI, Verse 15: "What will ye give me, and I will deliver him for thirty pieces of silver." Dearly beloved, you all know this account of the dreadful perfidy of Judas Iscariot, the betrayal of Our Lord Jesus Christ for a mere bagful of coins. What a transaction! A paltry sum for the life of the Son of God.'

Thomas had gripped the attention of the congregation, for they knew that he would give a new, personal twist to the old story. And so did I. After a pause, full of meaning, and looking round at the assembled villagers, he continued:

'Treachery on such a scale can happen only once in the aeons of mankind's life on Earth, for there has been only one Son of God made flesh. But…'

That word rang out; and again a pause – a long pause portending a message to be listened to intently.

'But,' he repeated, 'civilised people do revere their princes as having due to them a loyalty more deeply felt by their subjects, and more robustly hedged about with protection, than we expect of relations involving allegiances to persons below the majestic rank of royalty. In this country, a state second to none in the wisdom of its form of government and in the justice of its laws, our kings are anointed at their coronation ceremonies in order to symbolise their proximity to God compared with the lowliness of even their mightiest subjects.'

Another pause while he stared at his attentive flock.

Then: 'So, my brothers and sisters in God, do we not truly gauge treason as the most heinous of crimes, and treason against the person of our sovereign liege lord, the King, or his heir, the most heinous of this most heinous of crimes? Now, forgive me, for I sincerely mean no blasphemy: what would you say of a subject of our King, George III, who pointed out His Majesty, or His Royal Highness, the Prince of Wales for that matter, to a French assassin – in return for a pocketful of miserable francs?'

There it was, by Biblical and current political analogy! A veritable arrow shot into the conscience of the smuggler-conspirator we were trying to uncover and into that portion of his brain that triggered fear. Thomas had taken a perilous chance. He had obviously reckoned on the conspirator being intelligent enough to understand the near parallel between colluding with a French assassin and conspiring in an abduction, yet insufficiently suspicious to deduce that the vicar had learned of the plot and was alluding to it. Nevertheless, the gamble was a reasonable one. Whoever the smuggler was, the likelihood of his being able even to think of the possibility that his vicar knew of the plot, and that his sermon was a trap, was utterly negligible.

Thomas stared hard at the congregation. Because I had risen late – I bewailed my slothfulness – I had not had time to tell Thomas of my suspects. Nevertheless, during the service before the sermon I had been able to locate them in the congregation. The owner of the dominoes lowered his head as the vicar revealed the meaning of his sermon. And I could see that he was wringing his hands. It was Will Watson.

I knew him, and his poor family, of course. My exhilaration at my identification was immediately replaced with pity for him and compassion for his loveable wife and children. What a dreadful age we were living in!

That afternoon, before going to the camp again, Thomas invited me to eat with him. It was a basic though substantial meal of mutton, bread and ale. Naturally, I was eager to report that I was as certain as I could be that I had identified the smuggler-member of the little team of conspirators. He was as saddened at receiving this news as I had been when I had drawn my conclusion from Will Watson's reaction to the sermon.

After that I went yet again to the camp, as arranged. The colonel and the captain adjutant had worked out the details for the military-civic meeting. This assembly was to take place the following Thursday, the day after the punishments were meted out to the mutineers at Goldstone Bottom. Fifty soldiers of private and non-commissioned ranks would be marshalled in one of the parade spaces of the designed campsite, and about a score of civilians would be invited and provided with seats. The colonel was planning to visit leading citizens of Brighthelmston the next day, Monday, to explain the ostensible reason for the gathering and to secure names of those who would attend. These people included myself (representing Rottingdean), James and two other shopkeepers, an inn-keeper, the official known as the Master of the Ceremonies, a fisherman, the constable, the vicar (my friend Tom), a churchwarden, the vestry clerk, the town clerk, three or four of the commissioners responsible for the administration of the town, and a few undefined individuals who might be recommended by any of these. The time was set for three o'clock on the appointed afternoon. All of this was most satisfactory.

I took my leave and went back into the town to tell Tom and James about these arrangements. Both were highly pleased. James asked me to stay for a dish of tea, an offer that I unhesitatingly and gladly accepted.

After Mary had brought the refreshment in to the parlour, James said to me: 'Do you know what tomorrow is?'

I was bewildered as to the point of the question. I lamely said, 'Monday, 10th June.' That sounded so banal, so I made a joke: 'The day before St Barnabas' saint's day.' They were mildly amused.

'Ah,' said James, 'that may be so, but 10th June itself is Mary's birthday.'

I beamed at Mary, and said, 'I'm sure you are looking forward to that. How are you going to celebrate it?'

'I'm not sure,' she said. 'Could you perhaps spare the time to help me?'

'I certainly could, and would love to,' I responded, very obviously without the slightest delay.

'I'm so glad,' she replied just as speedily! 'It's a pity that the camp is only just becoming organised. The last two years, the parades and mock battles on the Downs behind the camp were highly entertaining spectacles; watching a repetition tomorrow would have been a perfect way to spend a large part of the day.'

'Yes,' I said, 'I have heard how popular these events have been, but, as I arrived in Rottingdean only last autumn and took some time to settle down, I have not had a chance to witness them myself.'

'You must not miss them this year, even though the mood

95

of the town is one of anger at the army for the treatment of those poor wretches so cruelly sentenced last week,' Mary said.

'Can you describe what happens?' I asked.

'That's rather difficult,' she said. 'For weeks on end there is a mixture of military training and civilian sightseeing. The soldiers provide colour by their uniforms and sound by the music of their bands, the shouting of orders, the explosions of gunfire and the pounding of horses' hooves. The crowds – the people of Brighthelmston and surrounding villages and towns, and visitors from further a-field who flock here in the summer months – provide another spectacle themselves. They arrive in every sort of vehicle from fashionable carriages to working carts, and wander, sometimes dangerously, through the camp and on to the areas where the displays take place.'

'Oh, dear,' I said, 'your birthday will have to be spent more sedately,'

'It's a shame, too, that the theatre doesn't open for another month yet,' James said to his daughter. 'But I do have a suggestion. A stroll round The Steyne would be very pleasant. Also, the Promenade Gardens and the Assembly Rooms have opened a little early for the season this year because of Their Royal Highnesses' visit, and every Monday there is a Ball at 'The Castle' Assembly Rooms. So, my idea is this. Ben will come here for luncheon, and then the two of you will have these strolls in the afternoon and, afterwards, go to the Ball. This will be a modest 'Undress' occasion, with no wearing of extravagant clothes and jewellery, because it is so early in the season. As part of my birthday present I will pay for you both, that is, sixpence each entrance to the gardens and six shillings each for the Ball, which includes tea or coffee! And, as the rest of my present, I will buy my lovely daughter a new dress and hat.'

'Thank you, father!' shouted Mary in great joy, standing up and leaning over to kiss him. 'It will be the most wonderful birthday I have ever had.'

I thought, what a wonderful present for me, too. I also thought, how fortunate it was that I had bought those new shoes. I said, 'that is too generous, James; let me pay those thirteen shillings as *my* birthday present to Mary. I must give her something as a token of our friendship.'

'Oh, thank you, Ben,' she said, kissing me on the cheek. James registered no annoyance at his daughter's forward behaviour: he evidently approved of this rapidly growing closeness. What a happy time it was!

'So,' said James to Mary, 'I had kept this a secret: I had intended to take you to buy a new dress from Mistress Haymes tomorrow morning. This can now be a ball-gown.'

Mary was glowing and shed an emotional tear.

The next morning I took especial care with my washing, shaving and dressing. Both Billy and Betsy seemed to sense my mood of relaxed happiness. At a suitable time I walked across to the vicarage to explain to Thomas my absence for the day, an absence not entirely related to my investigating activities. His look revealed total comprehension!

I left home to arrive in Brighthelmston at a time when James and Mary would have returned from their shopping. God was kind that day. The rain held off and the sun peeped through the ever-present clouds on occasion. The greyness of the sky was offset by the predominantly light blue of the ensemble Mary chose for her birthday presents; though they also showed touches of fawn. James joked that his daughter was displaying by this choice political allegiance to the Whig Party, whose colours were blue and buff!

Mary said, 'I must therefore be extremely circumspect in whose company I wear my new dress: it will be most appropriate in the presence of His Royal Highness, the friend of Mr Charles James Fox. But, oh! Ben, is *your* allegiance to Mr Pitt's Tories?'

'I take little notice of the wrangles between political Parties,' I answered, and added, I hoped, gallantly, 'so I pledge my allegiance to the wearer of the dress, irrespective of the colours.'

Immediately I made that little speech, however, I regretted it. Was I trying to be verbally too clever? Had I crossed the delicate line from gallantry to presumptuous familiarity? I held my breath.

Mary smiled sweetly, dipped a little curtsy, and said, 'Thank you kindly, sir.'

Mary having left these fine clothes in her room to wear later at the Ball, we partook of some food, and, in the afternoon, left for our promenade. First to The Steyne (or Steine, as it was sometimes spelt), a popular open space. I had little knowledge of Brighthelmston, so Mary provided explanations.

'Is this not a pleasant place for walking?' she asked me.

'Yes, indeed,' I said. 'So carefully fenced about with wooden railings and the grass so well tended.'

'It hasn't been like this for long,' she said. 'Until about 20 years ago, so I've been told, there was a stagnant, water-logged patch over there in front of the Marine Pavilion. Also, the area has been used, probably for centuries, by the local fishermen to dry their nets. Then, gradually, the area was drained, those railings were erected and local people and visitors took to it for strolls in good weather.'

'And what about the poor fishermen?' I asked.

'Naturally,' she said, 'they were highly displeased, to put it mildly, though they have in fact persisted. We are lucky not to be tripping over the nets this afternoon.'

'But by whose authority were these changes made?' I asked.

'Come, I'll show you,' Mary said, leading me to a large notice. This read, in an utterly peremptory manner, that no one was to 'run any Foot, or other Race, on this Place, or *Fight*, play at Cricket, Trap or Ball, or any other Game or Games thereon'. It then continued: 'The Steine is now enclosed, there is FINE TURF, which is kept constantly mowed and swept every day, where Ladies and Gentlemen and their Children May walk with the greatest Safety and Pleasure; and care is taken to keep off all Beggars and disorderly

Persons.' It was signed by a certain Captain William Wade, over the title of the Master of the Ceremonies (a title I recognised from the colonel's list of townspeople to attend the meeting).

Another question for Mary: 'Who was this dictatorial person? He may have been the Master of the Ceremonies, but he certainly didn't stand on ceremony when he promulgated those rules!'

'Not only was,' said Mary; 'still is. As the town became increasingly popular for visitors of fashion, the various forms of leisure and entertainment needed to be organised. Mr Wade was appointed for this task. His main duties relate to the Assembly Rooms at 'The Castle' and the 'Old Ship' taverns. So, perhaps if it hadn't been for his work, we might not be attending the Ball later today!'

We then walked past 'The Castle' and beyond the Prince's Marine Palace to the Promenade. The flower beds and shrubs were beautifully laid out; I commented on them to Mary.

She said, 'Yes, it is a great treat to walk here, and we are lucky today that the gardens are not so crowded as they sometimes are – probably the uncertain weather explains that. Especially when a band of clarinets, horns and bassoons is playing here and there are firework displays, the whole scene is one of gay throngs.'

We spent a happy, leisurely time in these gardens, talking. We had had so little opportunity to be on our own together before that day.

'Do you have any ambitions?' Mary suddenly asked me.

'I have not really given any serious thought to that,' I admitted. 'I'm not the kind of person who plans, despite what I've been doing during the last fortnight. But since you ask, I would like to have my own parish, to settle there, leading a quiet and useful life in the company of a wife who would be content with a modest way of living. If I were to become conceitedly ambitious, I would love to write a book on the relationship between religious faith and modern scientific research. There! You've made me think it through.'

'It sounds idyllic,' Mary said.

'Tell me more about your reading,' I said, tactfully avoiding my most prominent thought that Mary should be that contented wife.

'As I have mentioned,' she said, 'I have great admiration for Mary Wollstonecraft, so my first name was well chosen! I have read quite a number of books written by female authors – novels, works offering moral advice and children's fiction. But no one, in England certainly, as far as I know, has written with such originality and depth of feeling about the status and role of women. I wish I could write as she does, but she has already said almost everything on the subject, and I know that I could not possibly match her.'

And so we enjoyed sharing each other's thoughts and promised that, once the kidnapping had been averted and Jonathan's murderer had been caught, tried and punished, we would find many occasions to talk so freely. That vow was taken as we arrived back at her home.

After Mary had changed into her new clothes, I escorted her, equipped with my sword-stick – to complement my attire rather than to arm myself for combat – to 'The Castle' Assembly Rooms. She looked beautiful; I was proud to be her companion.

My ill-informed assumption about Brighthelmston – ill-informed in sharp contrast to its becoming famous even on the continent – was of a small, provincial fishing town, with a veneer of fashionableness because of the sea-cure and sea-bathing and the imprimatur of the Prince of Wales. This mental picture rendered me utterly unprepared for the magnificence of the Assembly Rooms' Ballroom. Designed in the style of the great Mr Adam, the room is shaped in pleasing proportions of eighty feet in length and half that measure in width. Its decoration is breathtaking: a brilliantly painted curved ceiling and colonnaded recesses made gay with yet more paintings. Moreover, the gallery to accommodate the instrumentalists had been just as thoughtfully incorporated into the overall design of the room. I was not surprised when Mary told me, noticing my look of awe on entering the room, that many considered it the most elegant Ballroom in England.

I noticed, too, that she also was overwhelmed by the surroundings and I mentioned this to her.

'I have heard about this room and of the kind of people who attend these Balls,' she said, 'but I have never been here before. It is like being in a dream – a dream of unbelievable happiness; not just to be here, but to be here with you, my dearest Ben.'

I was about to say something; I don't remember after all these years what, and I'm not so sure I knew then. In any case, I felt so choked with emotion, I am uncertain that I could have said anything.

Mary saved me from causing an awkward silence by expressing a dampening worry: 'Yet, like so many dreams, I have a nasty premonition.'

'This cannot be,' I said, clasping her hand. 'Tell me, so that I can persuade you to dispel it.'

'Just look,' she said, 'at all those rich and fashionable people. I have never owned such a lovely dress as father has given me today; and yet, I cannot compare with these ladies adorned in the height of fashion, even though this is what is called an "Undress Ball" and these other ladies are not nearly so gorgeously dressed as they could be. I fear that I shall disgrace you.'

'Mary,' I said, hoping she would not think me too intimate, 'I cannot see anyone as handsome in the whole room as you. All the other ladies' clothes are extravagantly garish and out of place; only yours fit the elegance of the room. And you wear them with a beauty and grace of perfect harmony.' I could see that Mary was quite overcome, so I added, 'And what about your sombrely black-clad escort?'

It was, I am proud to say, a most apt interjection of humour, turning Mary's uneasy mood to gaiety; though it was true that

101

most of the other participants at the Ball were evidently ladies and gentlemen of some wealth.

We most enjoyed dancing the minuets, for their charm, especially Herr Mozart's compositions, for the refinement of the movement they require and because they are designed to be danced by just two. We did join in the social dances such as the cotillion, though Mary still felt the others despised our lowly status. Until, that is, the Prince of Wales arrived. The dancing momentarily stopped; he was warmly welcomed; and he walked round saying a few words to his friends. Including me! I introduced Mary, whose dress he admired – especially the colours, he added with a chortle of political appreciation. The mood changed. Other dancers now wished to know us. Such is the immediate power of snobbery; and Mary gained confidence – such is the power of a kind word from a stranger.

On the other hand, the simplicity of Mary's dress could scarcely have contrasted more sharply with the Prince's attire. The local newspaper, the *Weekly Sussex Advertiser*, described it so well at this time that I copied down its wording exactly. The journalist wrote as follows: 'A most beautiful cut velvet gala suit of a dark colour, with green stripes, and superbly embroidered down the front and seams, with a broad embroidery of silver flowers, intermixed with foilstones. Waistcoat, white and silver tissue, embroidered like the coat.'

We interrupted our dancing a few times in order to sit in one of the alcoves, rest and drink tea. In one of these interludes we were approached by a man whom Mary vaguely recognised. He introduced himself to her, in a distinctively French accent, as one of her father's customers. He was an *émigré*, his name was Pierre-Auguste, Chevalier de St Paul. He quietly explained that James had asked for his help in identifying the French conspirator, was glad to help and therefore pleased to make the acquaintance of *le vicaire investigateur*, as he called me.

'I think I may know who your man is. I have not told M. Preston yet because I am not completely certain,' the Chevalier confided. Mary and I became even more attentive. 'His name is Louis Lefebvre. He poses as a lawyer who had close connections with those clergy who refused to swear the oath of loyalty to the Republic. He claims that, fearing for his life after the massacre of prisoners in Paris jails in September 1792, he fled to this country. However, when I have conversed with him, certain details do not ring true. Not only that, but there have been stretches of time when I have not seen him. Maybe our paths have just not crossed. Or he has been to France. I am suspicious. I think that he might well be a secret agent of the French Ministry of Foreign Affairs.'

The Chevalier gave us M. Lefebvre's address. We thanked him profusely and I said I would look further into this highly plausible suggestion. He then took his leave of us with typically Gallic charm, kissing Mary's gloved hand and favouring me with a low bow.

I warned Mary: 'We must be careful. We don't know he is who he claims to be.'

'You are becoming extraordinarily suspicious yourself,' she said with a smile.

I agreed and said, 'but tomorrow I must visit Mr Pelham and ask him to send a messenger to Mr Dundas to ensure that his men check on M. Lefebvre.'

At the end of the Ball, Mary and I walked the short distance to her home. We had both enjoyed a wonderful day – a birthday Mary said she would never forget – topped by another piece of information to help us complete the picture of the abduction plot.

And James had learned of another item. After he had welcomed us back and had happily seen the obvious joy in his daughter's face, he explained that, in our absence, he had received a visit from High Constable Wigney. James was impatient to tell us: 'The constable reported that he had searched Ned North's cottage and, although he had not found Jonathan's watch, he had discovered the prints that the murderer had taken from his saddlebag.'

'That proves he was the murderer!' Mary shouted in her excitement.

'Not quite,' James replied, 'because, when questioned, he claimed that he had bought them cheap from a man he met in "The George". On the other hand, the constable and I agreed that we did not believe that story. It will be useful evidence when the culprit is brought to trial. At one point, the constable was all for arresting him for the assault on Mary. But he soon saw reason – that we wanted to gather more evidence for the bigger crime.'

In turn, Mary and I told James about the Chevalier de St Paul. James said that he was indeed one of two regular customers he had spoken to about the French conspirator, and in his case, felt so confident of his discretion that he had told him that I was entangled in an investigation that related to French spies.

I was not entirely happy that James had spoken so freely. However, I bade both him and Mary a good evening, leaving the daughter to tell her father about the rest of her time at the Assembly Ballroom.

Betsy's slow walk back to Rottingdean (she was tired) gave me plenty of time to think back over the day. There could be no possible doubt that Mary was happy in my company. I so wished that I could have asked her to marry me. That was not possible. We had known each other for only a fortnight and, apart from that, she needed more time to recover from her brother's death. In addition to these temporary considerations, there was the impediment of my tiny stipend: I could not at that point in my life support a wife. Should I therefore cool down our growing relationship, or explain all this?

When I arrived home, a note had been left by Thomas asking me as a matter of urgency to call on him.

Chapter 10

Thomas handed me a note from two men who had tried to find me that afternoon. These were William Wickham and Evan Nepean, whose names the Prince had mentioned when Mr Pelham and I visited him at Windsor Castle. They were staying at the 'Old Ship' hotel and they were summoning me to see them without fail at eight o'clock the following morning. This contact by men of the government meant that I had no need of visiting Mr Pelham; I could report the conversation about M. Lefebvre direct to these gentlemen, experts in espionage in France and activities against French spies in Britain.

So anxious was I not to be late that I arrived early, after another miserable, dank ride. Even the windmill just beyond Ovingdean at Black Rock looked like a gloomy drenched giant, his arms outstretched imploring the sky for dry wind. Although I arrived before my appointed time, Messrs Wickham and Nepean were already in the foyer awaiting my arrival. Mr Wickham introduced himself and his colleague and led us to his room.

He was the first to speak. 'We are extremely pleased to see you, Mr Sydenham,' he said, 'and we convey the sincerest gratitude of our Ministers for your most speedy and highly intelligent work in this grave matter thus far. You, no less than anyone else apprised of this matter, know how little time we have; so, forgive our dispensing with pleasantries, and let us get down to business. Nevertheless, my presence here needs an explanation. You know from the Prince about my recent

105

and current work. By lucky chance I happen to be in England now for discussions with my recent colleagues in the Aliens Office.'

'Thank you for your kind words, Mr Wickham, and for your explanation,' I said. 'I am all too well aware that the attack on Marlborough House is set for eleven days' time. However, before you explain the detailed reasons for your and Mr Nepean's presence here, I must bring you both up to date with information I have only very recently acquired.' I told them about the constable's clue seemingly confirming Ned North as both conspirator and murderer, and the name of Louis Lefebvre as the possible Frenchman, and his address.

'Excellent!' said Mr Nepean. 'I refer to your mention of M. Lefebvre. Please forgive us. We know something of your heart-felt determination to ensure the conviction of Mr Jonathan Preston's murderer. And we truly wish you complete success in this endeavour. None the less, the concern of Mr Wickham and myself is the French connection with the plot against Their Royal Highnesses.'

'Yes,' I agreed, 'I fully appreciate the priority of your duties.'

'You are extremely understanding,' said Mr Wickham. 'Let me explain our responsibilities.'

Mr Nepean interrupted: 'We must not forget, Wickham, that Mr Sydenham will have little knowledge of the background and context of our operations,' he said.

'No knowledge at all,' I interrupted, eager to gain some.

Mr Wickham said, 'Of course, no reason why you should. Our work is exceedingly complicated. Since I have worked both in England and on the continent, perhaps it is I who should try to explain as succinctly as possible.'

It sounded more of an assertion than a question; but Mr Nepean nodded, and Mr Wickham instantly launched into his brief lecture.

'I can take it for granted,' he said, in a tone of voice that made me wonder whether this might be a question. But on instant reflection, I realised he could not conceive of anyone being ignorant of the basic facts he was about to expound. He did take it for granted that I was completely aware – 'that the safety and stability of this country since the outbreak of the French Revolution and subsequent war have been, to a severely worrying degree, threatened by a possible internal upheaval fermented by the perverted French political ideas, supported by secret agents crossing the Channel, and by a potential invasion of these islands.'

I indicated my understanding of these dangers. They were common knowledge and the causes of widespread fear.

'Mr Pitt,' he continued, 'has striven with his characteristic energy over the past six years to increase the strength and efficiency of our spy network in France and our defences against French spies in this country. Both Mr Nepean and I are proud to claim some credit for organising our secret agents in France.'

'I am confident that you have been operating a highly successful essential service,' I said. Mr Wickham's face was a struggle between acknowledgment of praise, contempt for a banal observation by an ignoramus in his field of expertise and irritation at being interrupted.

'Thank you kindly,' he responded somewhat curtly. 'Last autumn, he continued, 'I transferred to the Home Department to set up there the Aliens Office. Its purpose is to interview refugees in order to discover if they are *bona fide* or likely fomenters of trouble with our own Radicals – even of revolution in the French manner. Though I am currently seconded to the Foreign Office.'

'I had no idea that circumstances were so serious,' I admitted. 'You think, therefore, that the involvement of M. Lefebvre – if he is indeed the Frenchman plotting with our three Englishmen – has more sinister, political, motives, not just the ransom money?'

'Exactly,' replied the two espionage experts in unison.

Mr Nepean then assumed the task of explanation. 'The situation is particularly dangerous and delicate at the moment,' he said.

'You mean, the successes of French vessels attacking our ships in the Channel?' I asked.

'That is one perilous element of current concern,' he replied. 'You know about these events, do you?'

'We are all very conscious of the increased activity in the Brighthelmston area recently. For a start there was that audacious capture by a French cutter of a sloop and a brig early in the year. And further vessels taken by the famous *Eagle*, not to mention the capture of the valiant Captain Sydney Smith and his ship, all add up to an air of trepidation here,' I said, 'though we are grateful that the frigate *Diamond* is stationed off Brighthelmston for our protection.'

'And don't forget that English smugglers and French sailors are often working together: we know, for example, that the *Eagle* is operated mainly by English smugglers,' Mr Nepean added. He continued: 'But these local incidents must be placed in a broader context – as the various departments of government are of course doing. I must tell you that our continental allies are withdrawing from the war and there is strong pressure in Parliament, even from the Prime Minister's friend Mr Wilberforce, for Britain to follow suit. At the same time, discontent and demands for reform are growing apace throughout the country. His Majesty's government is nevertheless determined to prosecute the war against republican France unremittingly with the object of restoring the King, that is Louis XVIII, now that the poor young Dauphin has died. But what if the real purpose of the kidnap plot is not to extract money – assuredly too banal – but to demand as the price for the release of Their Royal Highnesses Britain's ending hostilities with France!'

He paused for me to digest this information and dreadful speculation. But I was able to tell him that the Prince had already suggested to Mr Pelham and me that this could be the likely aim of the plot.

He resumed: 'What I am about to say now I tell you in the strictest confidence. You will know that the royalists and other counter-revolutionaries are putting up a vigorous fight against the French government in the west, in Brittany and the Vendée region notably. A small army of *émigrés*, and – I think inadvisedly – a few released prisoners of war, will shortly be sailing from Southampton, escorted by British warships, bound for the Quiberon peninsula on the south coast of Brittany. Some four thousand troops in all will be landed to help the anti-republican activities there.'

Mr Nepean paused again. The look he gave me indicated quite plainly that the most significant item of information was yet to come.

He then said with deliberation: 'That military and naval force will sail next Monday, 17th June.'

The day of the planned kidnap. Was it a coincidence? Surely not; the secret of the expedition must have been kept ineffectually.

'I thank you, gentlemen, for expounding these matters to me so lucidly,' I said. 'Have you another reason, perhaps, for visiting Brighthelmston?'

'Indeed we have,' said Mr Wickham. 'As soon as we learned of the developments here, the two of us met. We agreed that the plot was much too daring and would require too careful planning to have been devised by a soldier, a coastguard and a smuggler. It had all the hallmarks of a design cunningly drafted by the French secret service. We sent top priority orders to our agents in this county – oh, yes, we have men here! – and in Paris, Rouen and Dieppe to gather what information, gossip or hints they could.'

'Luckily,' Mr Nepean added with a confident grin, 'I have a most able man in the office of the Vigilance Committee in Rouen.'

'How very useful,' I said, 'though I imagine it is too early for you to have received any replies just yet.' Mr Wickham agreed.

'Two other questions come to mind,' I continued. May I ask them?' Mr Wickham assented.

'My first,' I said, 'is: why are you making so much effort; do you fear that the precautions that have been devised to protect Their Royal Highnesses are insufficient?'

'No, not at all,' Mr Wickham assured me. 'We have discussed these in London with great thoroughness and let the Prince know of our approval. It is a risky plan, but combines all the required objectives quite admirably. Our concern rather is to use this plot for our own purposes: to discover beforehand what political demands the French government might make for the release of the royal personages. As Mr Nepean has already mentioned, we guess that the motive is the ending of the war. We desperately need to know if we are right. We also want to identify the French agents in both countries who are master-minding the plan.'

'What is your other question?' Mr Nepean enquired.

'It is a simple one,' I said: 'Why are you taking me, a poor, young, inexperienced country curate, into your confidence?'

'And our answer is also, basically, quite simple,' Mr Nepean said, with just a hint, perhaps, of a reluctant smile. 'We need your services.'

I raised an inquisitive eyebrow, and Mr Wickham explained. 'We want you to help us track down both ends of the French involvement in this plot. You have virtually identified your three English conspirators and in doing so know more about this matter than anyone else; what is more, you made a favourable impression on the Prince, who consequently has confidence in you.'

'That is most gratifying,' I said, 'and, naturally, I shall continue to assist in any way I can. Do you have specific suggestions as to how I might help?'

'Very much so,' Mr Wickham unhesitatingly replied. 'We want you to change out of your clerical dress and wear old ordinary layman's clothes so that you can engage unobtrusively in two activities. We do not wish you to be recognised in these exploits. I have some suitable garments here. Today I would like you to accompany me to a number of addresses in

110

Brighthelmston, posing as my assistant. There are houses where French men are living and about whom we have suspicions. You will be glad to know that one of these addresses is the house occupied by the man we believe is your Louis Lefebvre, though we know his real name is Lemaître. I shall introduce myself as an official of the Aliens Office and explain that I am checking that our records are up-to-date. You will stand behind me as inconspicuously as possible, pretending to take notes. In fact I want you to look carefully at each of these men so as to be able to recognise them again: really do take notes or sketches of their features if you think these will aid your memory. Later in the day you will describe them and where they live to your acquaintances who are privy to your plan, so that they as well as you, when you resume your clerical appearance, can look out for them.'

'I shall feel embarrassed at such a subterfuge,' I said, 'but it is in a most worthwhile cause, and I will do my best. However, you told me that you require my help in disguise for a second activity. What is that?'

'This evening' – it was now Mr Nepean's turn – 'I would like you to come with me to Normandy.' It was quite impossible for me to hide my startled look.

'I apologise for springing this upon you, Mr Sydenham,' he said in reaction to my facial expression. 'I must stress at once that you have every right and much reason to decline our invitation...'

A nice choice of word, was my immediate reaction.

'Some risk is involved, it cannot be denied, but I and my most excellent man in the region we shall be visiting will ensure that you are protected as far as possible...'

Those last five words at least had the ring of honesty.

'The plan is this: we take a fast coastguard cutter from Brighthelmston, avoiding Mr North's Greenway station, to a river inlet on the Normandy coast, where we shall meet my Dieppe agent. I want the three of us to exchange information and ideas. We return Wednesday night. The hazards are interception by the French at sea and on land. For the crossings we shall be escorted by HMS *Diamond*. In Normandy we shall have the protection of two small groups combined. One will be a motley collection of French men disillusioned with their government, and whose disaffection is strengthened with gold, a currency more dependable than the uncertain French franc; the other, both French and English smugglers whose only interest is to preserve their trade, which – ahem – I have promised not to impede.'

'You have evidently thought through and organised these arrangements with exemplary thoroughness. I cannot in all conscience decline to collaborate,' I said. 'I make two requests. The first is that I must inform Dr Hooker and Mr and Miss Preston that I shall be engaged in these tasks. The second is that, on our return from France, I shall be conveyed back to Rottingdean in time to sleep and then, on Thursday, to go to the army camp for the meeting of which you are aware.'

'You have our assurance on both counts,' said Mr Wickham.

I went direct to the Rottingdean vicarage. Thomas listened intently to my retailing of my meeting at the 'Old Ship', nodding his understanding and approval.

'There is just one problem,' he said. My heart sank. What had I not considered?

'You can't return to Brighthelmston now alone,' he said; and he saw my worried puzzlement. 'You cannot possibly leave Betsy there while you are away. I will look after her in your absence and I will take you in my phaeton to Brighthelmston.

How could I have been so thoughtlessly inconsiderate? My conscience and sudden awareness of my limited sense of prudence nudged me into thinking of Mrs Heath, in whose cottage I lodged, and Billy, who lodged with me. I explained to Thomas that I must sort out this difficulty.

'You certainly must,' he said. 'In fact, explaining your absence is the chief difficulty. The villagers have already been asking why such a conscientious young curate as you has been so frequently absent recently.'

Something else I had not thought of, let alone worked through for all this time. I was flustered in giving Thomas more apologies for my irresponsibility.

'You mustn't reproach yourself, Ben,' he said. 'You have had an enormous amount on your mind, and you can't expect to think of everything. Also, I have not wished to burden you even more with this little matter. Whenever the subject has cropped up I have, not to beat about the bush, told a lie, a sin from which, I feel in my heart, the good Lord will absolve me. I have said that the Rev Hudson has had need of extra help in Brighthelmston for a few days. One of our flock said that he knew you were friends and another said that he had seen you in Brighthelmston twice recently and now understood why.'

'That was most kind and ingenious of you,' I said. 'Thank you very much. It happens, as you probably know, that John Dring, Tom's curate, has been increasingly distracted and worried about the duty he is to perform tomorrow at the army punishment ceremony at Goldstone Bottom. Therefore, those who are aware of this would not be surprised if I was helping in the vicarage.' (In fact, that day he was to have a nervous collapse, from which he never recovered: quite dreadful.)

As I walked across to the cottage I pondered on how I was to explain my absence overnight to Mrs Heath. I too decided that I must descend to telling a falsehood as a sin quite venial in comparison with the powerful virtue of keeping fast the secret of our devices to protect our royal family and our country.

'Mrs Heath,' I said, as I entered the kitchen, where I knew I would find her. 'I have a favour to ask you.'

'Whatever it is, it will be no trouble to me and I shall be only too pleased to help you, Mr Sydenham,' she said.

'You have, I am sure, been aware that I have been away from Rottingdean rather often recently. With Dr Hooker's consent, I have been helping the Rev Hudson in Brighthelmston. I should have told you, but I have been so busy. And you, dear Mrs Heath, are too discreet to ask. Well, I have now been called away for rather longer. I have received a message that my mother has been taken ill. So I am travelling to Oxford to see her. I don't expect to be away for more than one night. Dr Hooker has agreed to look after Betsy and to take me to Brighthelmston for the coach to London. But I wonder if you would look after Billy for me?'

'Bless you, Mr Sydenham, of course I will,' the good widow said. 'We get on splendidly, as you know. I do hope that your mother is not too poorly.'

'No, no, I, I don't think so,' I stuttered in my confusion; 'but I do think that I should see her.' I then hurriedly left. However, not without taking the kind of bag I would have needed for that pretended journey, not to mention my sword-stick for the real one.

On our journey to Brighthelmston I confessed to Thomas my worry that I was neglecting my parish duties so. Thomas reassured me that he was still most happy to compensate for my absences, and that the present crisis in which I was involved would soon be resolved.

When I left Thomas I called on James and Mary. Unfortunately for me, James was in conversation with a garrulous customer who was negotiating a number of purchases, asking an inordinate number of questions, and wanted to gossip at length. I could not seek out Mary behind the shop without the customer, I was sure, asking at length about our relationship. I was on tenterhooks.

James comprehended the difficulty and, interrupting his financially valuable customer, said, 'Good morning, Mr Sydenham, so pleased to see you. Do please browse while I deal with this gentleman's requirements.'

I had not, as it happened, ever perused James's stock: I had always had other interests on my mind! If I had not been in such a hurry, I would have enjoyed the leisure of inspecting the shelves of books. At last, the customer, taking the hint, left with his bundles.

James called Mary and I explained to them my meeting with Messrs Wickham and Nepean.

'This is a noble and courageous undertaking you are embarking upon,' James said. 'We wish you every success.'

'When we see you next we expect a vivid account of this adventure,' Mary said.

I walked the few yards to the 'Old Ship' to prepare myself for my *incognito* activities, first in Brighthelmston, then in France. A feeling of nervous excitement was creeping into my consciousness. I went to Mr Wickham's room, knocked, and was invited in a clear voice to enter. We shook hands, and he asked if I had encountered any problems. I explained, somewhat shamefacedly, how Dr Hooker had rescued me from two difficulties.

'He is clearly a thoughtful and intelligent man,' Mr Wickham said. 'You are lucky to have him as a friend and confidant. Now, to business.'

He handed me some well-worn clothes for me to change into (from Mr Cobby's shop, I wondered?). I removed my own outer garments and dressed myself in those that best approximated to my size. The shoes were not comfortable!

'Put on that hat and pull it down over your forehead and pull up your coat collar,' Mr Wickham instructed. 'The less your face is seen the better... Yes, that's good. Now look at these lists.'

There were seven names, including Louis Lemaître (or Lefebvre). Their addresses were, naturally, all in Brighthelmston, though some of poorer appointment than others. In addition, the papers contained annotations – as much information as Mr Wickham had been able to assemble. This included: place of origin in France, stated reasons for emigrating to England, family relations, connections in England, continued connections in France. He handed me a notebook and pencil. We then set forth.

Our plan was complicated because only three on our list were at home. For the others, we asked neighbours, who suggested where we might find them. Even so, we failed to track down one of them. During the interviews, I jotted down notes about each man's appearance and, after leaving, privately made a quick sketch of the face that would have made any of our famous portrait painters shudder. Luckily the Frenchmen we had interviewed were all very different – in height, girth, colour of hair, age, shape of nose and so forth. We returned to the 'Old Ship'. I changed back into my own clothes and then walked to James's shop to hand over my notebook. He glanced at my descriptions and sketches quickly, jabbed his finger at M. Lemaître and said, 'that's the one I saw with the soldier in 'The George'.'

I took my farewells rapidly, Mary worriedly instructing me to take great care. Back again to the 'Old Ship' to resume my disguise.

Chapter 11

Mr Nepean was in Mr Wickham's room. 'Bring your belongings to my room,' he said, as he opened the door when I knocked.

I gathered up my bag, stick and clothes of disguise. Mr Nepean looked out to make sure that no one was in the corridor and swiftly ushered me into his room.

'Where is Mr Wickham?' I asked.

'You will not be seeing him again,' said Mr Nepean, 'he has gone to visit the constable to instruct him to cease his investigations of the murder for the time being: we don't want him to arrest or even frighten Mr North. Mr Wickham will then return to London. I shall be looking after you from now on.'

'Can you give me any more information, instructions and advice now?' I asked.

'First of all,' he said, 'I am glad to see that you are equipped with a sword-stick. Be sure to take it with you this evening. As I have said, we have good friends waiting for us, but most of the local people are not so friendly. They are only too aware of the centuries of war between our two countries; they have a considerable dislike of the English, apart from the smuggling fraternities, of course. It is best to be prepared, just in case.'

Another of his telltale phrases: 'just in case'!

'But what do you have in that valise?' he enquired.

I told him about my untruthful story to Mrs Heath to explain my absence, and said that, in any case, I needed to shave.

'I'd rather you didn't until we return,' he said. 'The scruffier

117

you look the better. I would like you to change again into the garments you will now be wearing and take some rest. Sleep if you can; you won't have much opportunity tonight. I shall arrange for food to be brought to our room at six o'clock. We are due to sail at seven, so that we arrive at the deserted mouth of the little river Saane, some eight miles west of Dieppe, in darkness. Our friends will have horses for us, and we shall ride the ten miles to a small village to the inn there, where the host can be trusted and has been warned to expect us. We can have our meeting after refreshment and rest.

Mr Nepean grinned, took a bottle and two large glasses from a small table and poured generously gauged drafts of a deep ruby wine, handing me one. 'Now let's just chat,' he said.

I first of all told him about James's recognition of M. Lemaître. This pleased him a good deal. Then we talked most convivially about our lives and interests. After a while, despite my protests, he recharged our glasses. After we had emptied them, he suggested that I lay on the bed to rest – suggested? – well, kindly ordered! Unexpectedly, it was not long before I started to feel drowsy. 'A reasonably fit man should not be sleepy at this time of the day,' I said to myself.

Through my fuzziness of mind, I started to worry. Had this Mr Nepean drugged me? Was he who he said he was? But he knew Mr Wickham. Were they both impostors? Was I being kidnapped because I knew too much about the conspiracy? Was I to be taken to France to, I knew not what, fate? Never to see Mary again?

He interrupted these hazy, frightening thoughts: 'I forgot to tell you. You must know that the Prince of Wales has – what shall I say? – has a most developed sense of humour. He told me how you and Mr Pelham drove frantically up to Clarence House, only to discover he was at Windsor! The way he told it, it was funny; though, of course, from your point of view, there was no humour in the journey.'

I relaxed. I now knew that this man must be Evan Nepean,

the man he claims to be, the knowledgeable, skilful, passionately loyal operator of Britain's extraordinarily complex and efficient spying operation in France and defender of the country against French spies. His Royal Highness would not, by any stretch of my distorted imagination, have talked in such a way to anyone who was a stranger. The explanation for my somnolence was much simpler and quite innocent. Mr Nepean *wanted* me to sleep, so that I would have my wits about me during the crossing, the ride to our destination for the meeting. He shrewdly assessed that the head of a poor young curate, the son of a poor don, was (since perhaps occasional undergraduate excesses) used to nothing stronger than small beer and weak communion wine. The potent vintage he had plied me with was bound to have a dampening effect on my consciousness.

I giggled – a reaction to my alcoholic condition, the realisation of the stupidity of my initial interpretation and contentment at my arrival at what I was convinced was the truth: as Pliny wrote: '*in vino veritas*'. And if truth and wine are so closely related, what a wonderful justification for a priest – or such a one as I who is a philosophical seeker after truth – to drink the beverage for enlightenment.

Mr Nepean inevitably heard my tittering. I explained. He laughed. And I soon collapsed into the arms of Morpheus. (How many times have I read that phrase? I wonder: is it a curse of a classical education that such metaphors are repeated to boring staleness?)

True to his word, Mr Nepean roused me shortly before six. The meal was most palatable – a goodly supply of mutton-chops (from, I wondered, the Downland denizens of Rottingdean?). At a quarter-to-seven, my guardian-companion making certain that the coast was clear, we left his room and walked out of the hotel by the back door. We made our way to the path past the chalk cliff in front of the building and so to the shore. The cutter was standing a little out to sea. Mr Nepean led me to a small rowing boat, by means of which we reached the coastguard vessel. Our boat was pulled up: we were going to need that for reaching the Normandy coast.

We were welcomed aboard by the coastguard officer in charge and taken to his small cabin, while his crew got the vessel under way.

Between them, the master of spies and the coastguard officer explained the procedure. Mr Nepean and I were to stay in the cabin out of sight, at least until darkness: no one from any other ship that might approach us should think that there was anybody aboard but uniformed coastguards going about their normal duties. The weather was perfect: thick cloud so that it would be dark early and no moonlight, helping us to avoid detection; and a brisk wind helping us to make good speed.

Some miles out we would meet *Diamond*, our escort. Both she and our cutter would carry dim lights. We would follow her, and in the event of any other ship being seen, *Diamond* would signal us to move to her side, away from the oncoming ship. Thus, if the ship was sailing east and therefore approaching our port side, we would move up to our escort's starboard side, to be invisible to the vessel approaching us and be protected from her if she was French.

By good fortune, in fact, we were not required to make that manoeuvre. I was nevertheless impressed at the care with which this operation had been thought through.

The crossing was an eerie experience. Pitch black – apart from the tiny pallid red and green lights on the *Diamond*'s stern before us – and the only sounds, the lapping of the waves and the movement of the rigging and of the sails catching the wind. Even these noises were only just audible in the cabin. Of human voices, there were none. It was the men's eyes and ears that were being used with the utmost concentration, hoping and praying that neither of these faculties would detect anything but the open sea.

As we approached our destination, we pulled away from *Diamond*. She did not want to draw attention to herself. And as we came near to the coastline, I had another uncanny experience. A sudden chink in the cloud allowed a glimmer of moonlight to escape. I strained my eyes to look at the scene. I thought I must be peering at the Sussex chalk cliffs, even to the undulations and gaps scored by rivers. It was as if Nature had placed a great mirror on the other side of the English Channel, and I began wondering about the reason for such similarities. I was given no leisure to pursue these musings.

Mr Nepean started to talk quietly: 'It is now time for us to install ourselves in the rowing-boat and make for that flashing light.'

He pointed in a direction a little way to our right (or should I say, 'starboard'?).

He continued: 'From now on it is imperative that we make as little sound as possible. Our rowlocks have been muffled with cloths and so will be the hoofs of the horses we shall be riding. Above all, do not speak unless it is absolutely essential, and then in a whisper. Not only must we avoid discovery on our journey to the inn, but I imagine your limited command of French and particularly your accent would alert anyone who heard you that you are English.'

I quietly agreed to that assessment, feeling a bit like a chastened schoolboy.

We rowed the boat into the mouth of the river and drew up to the western bank. As we alighted, four men immediately appeared like *dei ex machina* to haul the boat into a well-chosen hiding-place. One then returned to lead us fifty yards or so where a fifth man was waiting with seven horses. Mr Nepean went up to him and shook his hand firmly – I assumed this was his Dieppe agent. We were all soon mounted and we rode off, I gripping nervously both reins and sword-stick. Not a word passed anyone's lips, and the horses padded softly on the path and thence to a narrow rough road.

Our progress was slow, not daring to hurry because of the lack of light to guide us over the treacherously uneven road and for fear of making a noise. The ten miles, or thereabouts, to the village seemed like a multiple marathon. At last, we reached the inn, *Le Bergère heureux*. The happy shepherd. Another reminder of Sussex, and therefore a good omen? In Rottingdean, we had at that time a most remarkable shepherd-boy named John Dudenay, then thirteen years of age. He was already an avid reader, studying while tending his flock. He was helped and encouraged in his studies by Dr Hooker.

We went directly to a large shed to stable our horses. On entering the inn itself we were welcomed by the innkeeper. Our escort were sent off to a room upstairs with bottles of wine and promise of food later. Mr Nepean, his agent, known simply as 'Dubois' (a bilingual Englishman descended from Huguenot refugees), and I sat round a table, also furnished with wine.

Mr Nepean explained his plan. Our host would be bringing us food very shortly and after we had taken our refreshment, we would be shown to a room where we could sleep briefly. Later that morning, a British agent from Paris, known as 'Fabre', would join us for our 'council of war', as Mr Nepean called our meeting, only half in jest. We would start on our return journey, if the night was dark, at ten o'clock; if the cloud was scattered, allowing light, an hour later. We would arrive in Brighthelmston on the Thursday morning, in good time for me to change my clothes, be taken back to Rottingdean, rest and return to Brighthelmston for the civic-military congress, in Mr Nepean's grandiose term.

We had a substantial, convivial meal, lit by a limited number of candle-lanterns, after which I slept very soundly for a few hours. When I rose, the sun was up, of course. I discovered that the facilities for ablutions, which in darkness I had thought primitive, transpired, in daylight, to be quite nauseous. Also, the main room, where we took our meals, I now saw, was grimy, to be generous. I whispered a comment to Mr Nepean: he smiled and counselled me not to venture into the kitchen! Yet the innkeeper was friendly and considerate and his food was delicious. I pondered on the Baron de Montesquieu's thesis that different peoples have different cultural characteristics.

We were sitting, talking, having finished our temporally displaced breakfast, when Fabre joined us, and took a little refreshment. In due course, but with no sense of haste or impatience, Mr Nepean suggested that, since all four of us were assembled, we might start our meeting – in a private room.

He, inevitably, conducted our deliberations, with, I must say, exemplary proficiency.

'Gentlemen,' he started, 'first of all, on behalf of His Majesty's Government, I wish to thank you for attending this gathering, tiny in size but huge in the portent of its business. I have given some thought as to how best to use our time. We all know or have been fully informed about what has been happening in Brighthelmston since 27th of last month, so I need not waste time retailing that material. I believe that our agenda can be divided into three parts and together contain four problems, albeit of varying significance. I propose to list these three parts and relate them to the four problems. I would be most grateful if you would not intervene during my exposition. Thereafter, I will take questions for elucidation, receive and give up-to-date information, if there be any, then – our main purpose – discuss ideas about tackling the problems. Would this be satisfactory?'

We all assented. It was a most businesslike start of a businesslike meeting.

He continued: 'As I see it, we must be as sure as possible that we are completely prepared in the best ways to cope with three matters: namely, the planned Rottingdean diversionary landing; the main Brighthelmston, kidnapping landing; and what I shall call, for the moment, two miscellaneous questions. Let me summarise each of these in turn.'

We were not supplied with paper for taking notes – presumably he did not want to insult us by suggesting that we were incapable of understanding, absorbing, retaining and assessing his analysis. We concentrated on his every word.

'First, then, the Rottingdean feint,' our master-spy said.

'This must be allowed to go ahead and the conspirators must continue to expect a concentration of preventive officers there, drawn away from Brighthelmston. We shall not be interested in arresting anyone but the ringleader who, we have every reason to believe is one Will Watson. My hunch is that this gang will land innocent, legal cargo: what is the point of drawing attention to themselves and then being arrested by the overwhelming numbers they themselves have devised to muster? Probably most of the smugglers will be ignorant of the plot, but the lives of the likes of Mr Watson would not be worth living if it became known that the event was a trap.

'Here we come to our first problem. Ned North, the corrupt coastguard, has the duty of alerting the preventive authorities – Mr Jonathan Patcham overheard this and reported it to Martha Gunn. We must assume he has done this. Nevertheless, it would be prudent to have the message conveyed from a second source. I suggest that we must contrive for Will Watson 'accidentally', if you catch my meaning, to inform a coastguard or customs man. Yet he must do this in such a way as to incriminate himself, so that, when he is arrested, he can be successfully tried for complicity in the abduction plot.'

My admiration for Evan Nepean was growing. He had succinctly outlined this element in the conspiracy and pinpointed the key problem for us to solve.

After the briefest hesitation to give us a moment to digest this first part of our agenda, he went on.

'Our second item,' he said, 'is, naturally, the heart, the primary theme of this drama. Their Royal Highnesses, it goes without saying, must be totally protected. On the other hand, in the course of that operation, we would not wish any of the kidnappers to escape. Some will inevitably be killed in their encounter with the bodyguard troops. However, both Mr Wickham and I, not to mention our Ministers, are exceedingly anxious to have as many as possible captured so that we may interrogate them before their trial and execution. We are most keen to know who in Paris – if that truly be the controlling origin of the plot – has been directing this operation, and if any *émigrés* in Brighthelmston, apart from our suspect, M. Lefebvre/Lemaître are involved. He therefore must be taken alive. How to ensure all this is our second problem.'

However worrying and complicated the murder of Jonathan and the protection of the Prince and Princess had seemed a fortnight earlier, how much more perilous and complex the affair was steadily being revealed in the context of the war with France.

'We have also my two miscellaneous items,' our chairman said. 'The first is firmly to identify the soldier and lure him, as with the smuggler, to reveal his part in the conspiracy. That is our third problem. And, finally, there is the issue of apprehending and bringing to justice the murderer. Strictly, this is not our responsibility; on the other hand, the crime appears so closely connected to the planned abduction that we really must not forget it. Furthermore, we owe it to Mr Sydenham, who is personally deeply involved in the case, to assist in every way we can. But, how? That is our fourth problem.'

The great expert on spying sat back. I broke the silence.

'I cannot add anything to that masterly analysis,' I said, 'except to report what I have already told Mr Nepean, namely, that yesterday my friend Mr Patcham recognised, from my notes on suspect *émigrés* in Brighthelmston, that Louis Lemaître was the Frenchman at the conspirators' meeting in the inn last week.'

'Excellent!' said Fabre. 'Could you, Mr Sydenham, give us a description and a sketch? We, on this side of The Channel must make our own enquiries. The details Mr Wickham gained from him about his background are almost certainly false, so there is no point trying to follow up that information.'

Mr Nepean then did produce pencil and paper. I did my best.

He then said, 'Well, now, if there are no more general comments, let us tackle our problems one by one. First, how do we handle Will Watson?'

Several suggestions were forthcoming, but none met all the requirements. These were, to repeat: that he should not have an inkling that he was being deceptively used; and that the manner in which he lets fall the information about the landing of the goods should not arouse the suspicion of the officer or officers who hear it but, by being heard, he will be incriminating himself. Dubois did not contribute to these abortive suggestions. His elbows on the grubby table, his fingers massaging his temples, and his brow deeply furrowed, he obviously grasped that it was useless to proffer an idea unless it satisfied these requirements. At last he spoke.

Releasing his head from his hands and gesticulating with his forefinger, the spy whom Mr Nepean had stationed in Dieppe explained his plan.

Turning to me, he asked, 'I am correct in understanding, am I not, that there is a customs house in Rottingdean and cottages for the revenue men?' I nodded. 'And there must be an inn.' I nodded again.

'Right. My idea is as follows. Tomorrow evening, you, Nepean, suitably attired and having been briefed by Mr Sydenham, will call on Will Watson, posing as a French smuggler involved in organising the plot. You will take him to the inn, instruct him that he must, as a matter of urgency, let the revenue men hear about the landing of goods on 17th – next Monday, I need hardly remind us. You will tell him that 'we' – that is, the French organisers – are not sure that Ned North can be completely relied upon, but that we believe that he, Will, can be – play on his conceit. Buy him plentiful tankards of ale. Then walk – he no doubt unsteadily – to the customs men's cottages, outside of which you stage a drunken argument, he assisted to verisimilitude in this behaviour by his alcoholic intake. During this exchange, taunt him in a loud voice that, because so many smugglers are involved, he won't be paid very much for his part in the operation. He, in turn, forgetting all caution, will, I wager, boast that he is the key organiser in Rottingdean. The residents of the cottage would not fail to hear the message!'

'It all fits, by Jove, it fits!' cried Mr Nepean jubilantly. We all congratulated Dubois. But could the other problems be solved as satisfactorily?

I intervened at this juncture, thinking aloud: 'I wonder if we could use the same kind of tactic with the soldier? If all goes well tomorrow afternoon we shall identify him. However, as with Will Watson, we must inveigle him into saying something that can be used as evidence at his trial.' I looked at Mr Dubois.

'I think it should be possible,' he said to me. 'Tomorrow afternoon, Mr Nepean could happen to be a bystander watching the meeting. When that is concluded he could wander in your direction and you point out to him our treacherous trooper. He would then approach the soldier and whisper that the organisers of the forthcoming "event" need to be assured that what he is devising will be successful, that his future will be in jeopardy if it is not.'

We all reacted merrily, clapped, and assured Mr Dubois that he was a most clever and ingenious fellow. Mr Nepean said that he would not have engaged him for his work in Dieppe or have arranged this meeting in France if he had not been so, and unhesitatingly agreed to the plan.

He then resumed his chairman's duty. 'To proceed,' he said. 'The problem of Marlborough House, let us call it, is more complicated and, I suspect, more difficult to solve.'

'I am very much an outsider,' said M. Fabre, 'so please tell me without equivocation if what I am about to say is useless.'

We encouraged him to carry on. I, of course, did not know him. Nevertheless, in our brief acquaintance, he struck me as a man of intelligence and common sense; more than that, when His Majesty's Government was constructing its network of spies in France, it was bound to allocate to Paris their most highly regarded agent.

M. Fabre continued. 'It seems to me, Nepean, from your admirable synopsis, that inside this problem, both complex and of cardinal importance, there lie two issues. One, is the avoidance of killing the key conspirators in Marlborough House; the other is preventing them from escaping.'

The three of us all nodded in agreement to this lucid simplification. All very well, I thought, but how do we achieve this? M. Fabre, of course, was about to tell us.

'It is therefore obvious, to take the first issue,' he said, 'that there must be present on the evening and night of 17th June at least one person who can identify the principal conspirators, most especially M. Lemaître, and to warn the soldiers at all costs not to shoot or wield their swords to kill them. Messrs Sydenham and Wickham can recognise M. Lemaître and Mr Sydenham can recognise Mr North, if his commitment to the plot involves him in the climax. I put it to you, therefore, gentlemen, that Messrs Sydenham and Wickham should both be present next Monday night at Marlborough House.'

In the silence that followed I was conscious that three pairs of eyes were focused on me. The meeting could not progress until I had reacted to Fabre's logically constructed plan.

With obvious hesitation and fear in my voice, I at last said, taking a deep breath and swallowing hard, 'Fabre is right. I cannot, of course, speak for Mr Wickham, but I believe that I have a responsibility to take part in the plan. I am neither spy nor soldier and the only courage I have I owe to my faith in Christ Jesus. I have no idea how I shall behave. You have my solemn word that I shall do my best.'

Another silence followed, much longer this time, while I worried that I was now pledging to place myself in danger, in complete and utter contradiction to Mary's wishes and plea when we parted.

Mr Nepean broke the quiet of those long moments. He said, 'Rev Sydenham, your country will be for ever in your debt.'

I felt most uncomfortable and stared at the dirty table in front of me.

Fabre then resumed. 'My most grateful thanks,' he said to me; then, addressing us all, 'We may now concentrate on my second issue. It is this: if the Prince's bodyguard are inhibited from killing, some of the would-be kidnappers might escape from Marlborough House. Indeed, as I shall explain, we *want* one or two to escape. They would obviously make for the boat waiting to take the royal captives to France. We need some men to lie hidden, waiting – in bathing machines, perhaps, – to ambush these fugitives. Now, my suggestion is as follows. Dubois should supply these men from his trusted helpers you have already seen. He and his men would sail to Brighthelmston the previous night. They would sail back in the kidnappers' vessel with the intention of meeting the French party waiting to receive the Prince and Princess. One of the reasons for taking some kidnappers alive is to find out from them – with expeditious persuasion – where the landing place in Normandy is to be.'

Mr Nepean said, 'My dear fellow, these are really splendid ideas; what do you think, Dubois?'

Dubois agreed, but added: 'It is absolutely essential that the commanding officer of the troops providing the bodyguard be fully informed about these requirements as soon as possible. A task for you, I think, Nepean, immediately on your return tomorrow. I suggest also that you ride to London the following day to recruit Mr Wickham for his part in these adapted arrangements in Marlborough House.'

Mr Nepean said that these were excellent ideas and suggested that we should pass on to our final problem. He asked me if I had any suggestions for proving the guilt of the murderer.

I said, 'This is difficult, therefore it is another reason for taking the kidnappers alive. We are assuming that the culprit is Ned North, so we must search him for Jonathan's watch. In the last analysis we need to persuade him to confess to the murder. He will know that for his part in the kidnap plot he will be executed, and for the sake of his conscience and soul, he might explain the reason for the killing of Jonathan, for we are at a loss to think of a really clear motive, let alone find firm evidence.'

Mr Nepean thanked me for that contribution. There were no other suggestions or queries. The meeting was concluded, enabling us to eat more food, to rest and to wait until darkness, when we could start our return journey.

Chapter 12

Having said our farewells to Dubois and Fabre, back to the coast the way we had come, again in dark silence. Our escort, Dubois, Mr Nepean and I had traversed about half the distance when, thinking about how out-of-character it was for me to be involved in such a dramatic and secretive venture, I realised that our escort carried no firearms – in order to avoid excessive noise in any encounter, I surmised. Our defence would be conducted by means of the blade. I tightened the grip of my right hand on my sword-stick.

As if my thought had some malign supernatural power, almost simultaneously we *were* attacked by a band of brigands on foot, themselves taking the precaution of silence and the advantage of darkness. One of these assailants grabbed my horse's bridle. Like a mindless automaton, in a flash, I triggered my blade and brought it down on his wrist. By good fortune, he had attacked me from the left, so my weapon had a powerful sweep. He shrieked and fled. I looked round. With expert tactics our guards had drawn their formidable cutlasses and sabres and put the rest of the ruffians to flight. Our attackers, expecting easy robbery, had not bargained on such deft defence and counter-attack.

Mr Nepean was immediately by my side, concerned for my safety. When I confirmed that I was unhurt, by virtue of the swift wielding of my sword-stick, he had to stifle a laugh – knowing how reluctant I had been to carry the weapon – and congratulated me by patting me on the shoulder. He then

131

instructed a faster pace, in case the brigands should return, using more artful tactics, or the noise of the encounter bring others to investigate.

When we arrived at the mouth of the little river we recovered the rowing boat, Mr Nepean and I waved our farewells to our escort and made our waiting coastguard vessel without further incident.

I, however, was shaken. Although I had suffered minor rough schoolboy unpleasantnesses (unpleasant for me, a pacific child), I had never before been viciously attacked, in circumstances in which I could have been seriously injured or even killed. That was frightening enough. But I had also learned something worrying about myself. I had lashed out in an uncontrolled frenzy. I was reasonably satisfied that I had given my attacker nothing more than a severe laceration. Even so, could I, in a different situation, and equally without time to take stock, plunge my weapon into a man's vital organs and kill him? I felt like throwing my sword-stick into the sea.

I dozed intermittently during the night crossing back to Brighthelmston, sleep constantly interrupted by these memories and worries. At first, in my waking moments, as so often happens during the hours in bed, I convinced myself that the purchase of the sword-stick had been wrong, an evil act, even. Then, after more periods of sleeplessness, I managed more balanced thoughts. If I had not been armed, I might have been quickly pulled from my horse in that ambush and been injured, possibly killed, before a member of our escort could have rescued me. This was the first time I had used my weapon; the next time I might not act in such panic. And the person whose judgment on moral matters I respected and relied upon most, Thomas Hooker, had advised me to arm myself in this manner.

We arrived at Brighthelmston early in the morning of Thursday, 13th June. I accompanied Mr Nepean to his room in the 'Old Ship'. I thoroughly cleansed myself after my gruelling adventure, shaved and changed, with great relief, into my own clothes. Mr Nepean took me to the hotel's stable. We had already arranged that I would ride his horse to Rottingdean; then, in the afternoon, I would return to Brighthelmston, mounted on Betsy, leading his horse to restore it to him.

Having surreptitiously left Mr Nepean's horse in the good care of Dr Hooker, collecting Betsy and promising to return with my news, I went home and ate a hearty meal. I then walked across to the vicarage to regale Thomas with my story. In the early afternoon I made the journey again to the 'Old Ship', returned the borrowed horse and then went on to tell my story again, this time to James and Mary.

Mary was horrified to hear of the brigands' attack; I thanked James for his expert instruction that had enabled me to fend off the man who had assaulted me. But, naturally, I concentrated on explaining in detail the plans we had devised in *Le Bergère heureux*. Mary told me that, in my absence, Jane Patcham had visited her to report that the soldier-guards were starting to be secretly installed in Marlborough House, according to plan.

It was then soon time for James and me to go to the meeting at the campsite. Benches were set out for the civilians, who were gradually arriving as James and I entered the field. We, as all the other townspeople, were welcomed by the colonel, and the adjutant led us to our allotted places. The front row had, inevitably by etiquette, been reserved for the civic leaders and the commanding officers of the two barracks.

The captain arranged that he would sit at the end of the second row with James behind him, I next to James. The adjutant's position did not seem contrived because, as we soon learned while the representative soldiers were marched in to stand opposite us, the colonel stood at our end to conduct the meeting. His adjutant was therefore to hand to assist his commanding officer if need be. The real purpose, as we had arranged, was that James could recognise the conspirator, tell the adjutant, who would, in turn, tell us his name.

The colonel welcomed the town's representatives and the barracks' commanding officers, explained the reason for the meeting and invited the army's 'guests', as he called us, to start the exchange of views. The Master of the Ceremonies, Mr Wade, spoke first – as was perhaps proper; but even if it was not, it was unsurprising that he felt he should start the discussion.

He said, 'On behalf of the people of Brighthelmston, I think that I should stress that the centres of entertainment, inns and shops have become dependent for their profits on the large numbers of visitors who come here in the summer and autumn. Indeed, these attractions and amenities have been expanded in recent years in order to cater for this welcome influx.'

These comments were supported by a bass chorus of 'hear, hears' from the benches.

Mr Wade smiled, half turned and executed a little bow, then continued. 'Because of the bad weather, the prospects, if it continues, will be a dampening of interest in visiting our resort this year.'

He waited for appreciative laughter for the double meaning of his carefully chosen word, 'dampening', which was, sycophantically, duly forthcoming.

'But, as you are well aware, sir,' he said, addressing the colonel, 'one of the major ...' (I shuddered, but then thought that *that* word was innocently used) ... 'one of the major attractions in most recent years has been provided by our gallant soldiery based in this camp. However, the horrified reaction to the court martial is likely further to reduce the number of our visitors.'

Renewed 'hear, hears'.

'Thank you very much, Captain Wade,' said the commanding officer, with excessive politeness, using the Master of the Ceremonies' military title, the validity of which was widely questioned. 'I cannot possibly, as you will appreciate, comment on the judgments of the court martial. Nor can I command the weather to improve!'

Oh, dear! That attempt at light humour met with no response. It was not, at least yet, a particularly amiable gathering.

'No, but you need not order us out to work when the weather is specially cold and wet,' came a voice from the ranks of the soldiers. 'There are no means of drying our uniforms in the tents after we have been soaked by the rain. We are not in the field of battle at the moment when we would expect to suffer these miseries. And I hope you won't court-martial me for making this complaint, sir.'

This interjection was followed by clapping and shouts of 'that's right', 'we agree' and indecipherable mutters indicating the unanimity and depth of feeling on this matter. The colonel bent down to engage in a whispered conversation with the adjutant.

He then said, 'I am sympathetic to what Private Yates has just said. We must, of course, have the camp ready when the units arrive. We had not expected the unprecedentedly foul weather conditions as late in the year as this. The adjutant and I have just agreed that we shall look at the programme again and try to arrange a relaxation of work on especially bad days.'

While these exchanges were taking place, James and I were looking for the persons we each wanted to see – though with the utmost care, lest we might appear not to be concentrating on the proceedings. I was delighted to notice Mr Nepean in a little knot of bystanders interested in or curious about what was happening. James glanced at me and gave an almost imperceptible shake of his head. He had not, to use the apt slang word, 'spotted' the conspirator in the rows of soldiers.

At that moment came another contribution from that direction. A soldier, standing in the back row, said, 'Sir, I would like to make a suggestion.' The colonel gave his permission for him to carry on. 'The reason for this meeting is to ensure that the soldiers and the townspeople understand each other and for the civilians not to feel quite so worried.'

An east wind had blown up and was carrying the voice of the soldier, unused to public speaking, away from us on the benches; indeed, many of us were cupping our ears in an effort to hear the barely audible voice. This man, I decided, was no drill sergeant!

The colonel, noticing this problem, said, 'Private Smith, I am sure that we would all like to consider what you have to say, but some of our guests are finding a little difficulty in hearing you. Come and stand here at the end of the front row.'

Private Smith: Silas Smith, the adjutant's favoured candidate to be the conspirator? My heart was racing and I exchanged glances with James. The said Private Smith could not possibly refuse to obey his commanding officer's virtual order. He came to the front. *His* front strained his belt – assuredly, the adjutant's aid to recognition, which he had described as 'a noticeable frontal protuberance'! I glanced at James, whose mouth shaped itself into a broad smile. It was his turn to have a whispered conversation with the adjutant, who kept a properly disciplined straight face.

But what had Silas Smith to contribute?

'I apologise, sir, for my quiet voice,' he said, 'I think it has been affected by the cold and wet conditions in which we have been working.' An outburst of laughter from the ranks; and, I must confess, I had some difficulty in suppressing a grin. He continued: 'What I want to say is this. There is one person in Brighthelmston who is both a member of the town and a soldier. That is, His Royal Highness Prince George. He rents the Marine Pavilion and has attended our camps.'

Loyal hurrahs from the ranks of both the troops and the civilians. Immediately I was suspicious. What was he up to? I nudged James and listened with utmost concentration.

Private Smith went on: 'My idea is that both us soldiers from the camp and barracks and you townspeople get together to hold a grand fireworks display and a concert of bands in honour of the Prince being here now. It would show everybody that there are no problems between us, that we all share the same loyalty. We should pray for dry weather, of course, and it will take a few days to arrange, of course, including the agreement of His Royal Highness. I suggest next Monday.'

That was it! My head nearly burst. The conversation Jonathan overheard involved Private Smith organising a diversion at least partially to occupy and distract all the soldiers in the town at the time of the abduction. Mutiny was unthinkable because of the recent court martial. Here was a seemingly innocent alternative. It also had the extra advantage of confusion and noise in the town, diverting anyone's attention from a gang acting in a manner that might otherwise look suspicious. The plan was ingenious; Silas Smith's presentation was masterly; he had evidently been coached – by the French. Because the following Monday – he could not have been more precise – was 17th June!

There were a few other contributions – by soldiers from the barracks and the townspeople, but I was not listening. The meeting came to a conclusion. The colonel thanked the representatives of the town, his fellow officers from the barracks and camp. He gave his assurance that he would discuss with the civic leaders and his fellow commanding officers Private Smith's suggestion.

We broke up. Mr Nepean 'happened' to pass me, and I whispered, 'Private Smith of the fireworks and concert'. I last saw our expert spy sidling up to the soldier. He was no doubt telling him that, unless his planned diversion was successful, he would regret it, and ensuring that the soldier implicated himself in the conspiracy by his response. Mr Nepean then melted into the crowd before Silas Smith could take a good look at him. No doubt, I thought, Mr Nepean would be visiting Rottingdean a few hours later to lay his trap for Will Watson.

James and I walked to his shop. We told Mary what had happened at the meeting, drank tea and agreed that there was nothing else to be done. Our mood was partly a sense of relief and partly a feeling of emptiness after so much recent sadness, worry, planning and activity. But we just had to wait. I left, to collect Betsy for the journey home. It had started to rain. Again. The soldiers were perhaps justified in complaining.

I spent the next day in conscience-stricken catching-up with my priestly duties, though I knew that Thomas had done sterling work in my many absences.

The day after that was Saturday. I woke with a vague sense of unease. I tried to pinpoint the reason over breakfast, but without success, to a certain extent because Mrs Heath wanted to chat. The morning, surprisingly, was dry and reasonably bright. I decided that what I needed was a long, solitary walk, for quiet contemplation after three such hectic weeks – to clear my thoughts, order my memories, calm my emotions and get things in perspective. I called on Dr Hooker, who was starting work on his sermon and explained my intention. He agreed most heartedly, thinking my idea a capital way of taking advantage of what promised to be a fair day.

I had given no thought as to where I would take myself. I started up the steep incline to the ridge of the sheep-clad Downs, looking out to sea, and tramped westward along the hills. My route took me on an undulating journey as the gentle curvature of the Downs rose and dipped, descending behind Brighthelmston itself as the valleys, providing the roads to London and Lewes, cut through the hills. And so I passed, on my right, the horse-race track, so popular with the Prince of Wales and his friends. From my elevated positions I looked down upon familiar sights – the fishing-boats on the sea, St Nicholas Church, the West Mill in Belle Vue field – all reduced to carefully crafted children's toys. Not to mention the toy soldiers working on the extensive campsite, stretching westward into the heart of the parish of Hove.

That gave me an idea. I would take as the terminus of my ramble the shamefully derelict Hove church of St Andrew, used at that time, as James had told me, only twice a year for services, but much more frequently for storing smuggled goods. As I neared the building I started my descent from the hills, and the soldiers working on that end of the campsite steadily grew to full size.

The church stands just beyond the northern end of the one street that is the village of Hove. I wandered round the outside, looking at the gravestones and becoming increasingly appalled that the western portion barely existed: there was no tower and many of the stones had been taken from the very fabric of the building, so in places it looked as if it had been chewed away by some huge lithophagous beasts (if I may use a word so appropriate for that condition, but which I have just learned as I write this narrative). I opened the creaking door to let myself into the intact part of the church.

Some light entered the nave from the dirty windows, though the appearance was one of pervasive gloom. I walked slowly through the nave. I became vaguely aware of a noise behind me. However, I was so intent on bewailing the state of this house of God that the sound barely registered in my consciousness. Eventually I turned round, but could see no one else in the dismal surroundings. I walked to the font and bent over to examine it.

I have no idea how long it was before I recovered consciousness. When I did, I was most uncomfortable: my head hurt, my wrists and ankles were tied, and I was propped in a sitting position against the font. As I focused my eyes, I saw standing before me the man who had obviously struck me and trussed me up. It was Silas Smith. He leered.

'I am very suspicious of you,' he said, 'and of your friend, the book shopkeeper. I've seen you visiting the camp; my friend, Ned North, saw the bookshop man spying on us in 'The George'; and I saw the two of you together, sitting next to the adjutant at yesterday's meeting. I spied you coming over the hill to the church, so I thought this would be a good time to have a little talk.'

His grimace was not a pleasant sight, nor his guffaw a pleasant sound. I was horrified that he and his co-conspirators had somehow worked out that we had discovered something about their plot. I was also terrified that he intended to do away with me. The throbbing pain in my head and my terror tugged my brain away from clarity of thought; the primal urge for self-preservation pulled it in the contrary direction.

The latter impetus gained an extra power by my sight of the tent-peg mallet, swinging menacingly in his right hand. That was clearly the weapon that had rendered me unconscious. Nevertheless, I struggled the best I could to summon some capacity for balanced, rational thinking. Accordingly, I deduced, in my dazed state, that he evidently wanted information from me or he would have killed me already. The mallet was also to be the means of extracting that detail. That lucid reasoning was directly confirmed.

'I want to know what you are up to,' Private Smith demanded, 'and I don't think you'll like what I'll do to you if you don't tell me.'

A cold shiver ran down my spine and my stomach sent a message of nausea. It was imperative that I fabricate a plausible tale avoiding any evidence of hesitation.

I tried to gain a little time by saying, in a slurred voice, 'It is rather complicated, and the pain in my head is so dreadful I don't know where to start.'

'Start anywhere you like, or I'll make your headache much worse,' he threatened.

'Well, let me try,' I said. 'You will have worked out from my clothes that I am a clergyman. And surely you know that clergymen want to help people to be good....'

Private Smith shouted, 'You're wasting time. Get on with it.' He emphasised this demand by waving the mallet near my left temple. I complied.

'I have become very distressed at the appalling punishments meted out to the poor soldiers at Goldstone Bottom. Rumours have been circulating that there might be a mutiny in Brighthelmston. I learned this from Mr Preston, the owner of the bookshop, as I have talked to him. I buy books of philosophy and science, you know: these are fascinating subjects. For example, did you know....' He wielded his mallet again. I continued my narrative falsehood, warming to my tale.

'I could not bear the thought of our local soldiers complaining, I am sure quite justifiably, about their conditions and suffering the same gruesome fate as those stationed at East Blatchington. Mr Preston agreed with me. We therefore tried, perhaps rather clumsily, to find out in what ways you were suffering, and hoped that we could persuade your officers to ease your conditions. Surely you must realise that yesterday's meeting is likely to be of benefit to you.'

I was very proud of myself. The unclouded and logical thinking I had been taught to develop as a student was paying off. My story was assuredly utterly credible; all the parts hung together.

The soldier looked at me and said nothing. Did he believe me? He was no doubt turning it over in his mind. Eventually he said, 'I don't believe you,' and raised his mallet.

'Please, don't be hasty,' I said, swiftly, at least to delay another blow. 'Would you strike a man of the cloth as recompense for what he has been trying to do in his own Christian manner to help you and your fellow soldiers? And why should I not tell you the truth? What possible reason can I have for lying to you?'

He again hesitated. Was he becoming convinced?

'Sounds all right,' he said. Another hesitation, as my heart beat furiously. 'So I shan't do you in. But I can't be too careful. If I let you go now, you'll get me into trouble – knocking a clergyman unconscious. How many years would I get for that? I couldn't even plead self-defence. I've got to keep you here for a few days. I'll bring you bread and water.'

He started to walk towards the door. He stopped and came back.

'I've got to shift you tonight,' he said. 'I've just remembered: tomorrow's Sunday; there'll be a service here and you'd be found.'

Not being a local man, he had no idea that the church was

effectively not used. He soon returned with a strip of cloth, which he bound over my mouth. Wherever he was going to hide me, he was evidently not going to take any chances that I might be able successfully to cry for help

Chapter 13

Silas Smith, then, was going to return after dark, drag me out
of the church and bundle me into some other hiding place. So
many consequent thoughts crowded into my mind that I
became confused. I took a deep breath to calm and control
my brain.

I started to think slowly and carefully. Mrs Heath would
be aware of my absence. Not necessarily that night – my
habits had become so irregular recently. However, I had never
been away overnight without telling her, and she would start to
be worried at breakfast-time when I did not appear. Even
more – Billy would by then become loudly vocal about the
absence of his food-provider. In all likelihood, when she
received no reply from her knocking on my door, Mrs Heath
would hasten across to the vicarage to tell Thomas of my
absence and he would organise a search.

But, I knew that, if there was any hope of one of my friends
finding me, I would needs be patient during the evening and
night. I began wondering if I could devise some desperate
clue to indicate my presence to any possible rescuers. It was
a hopeless thought. My hands were tied behind my back; my
ankles were attached to a rope, which Private Smith had bound
round a stone pillar; and my mouth was gagged. Moreover, if
anyone came looking for me in the church in the morning, I
would not be there, as the soldier had told me; and wherever
he would be moving me to, he was sure to render me equally
secure and mute.

Where would he be taking me? It was probably a place where no one else would think of looking. The chance of my being freed before the kidnap attempt seemed negligible. Silas Smith would be arrested, and I considered it unlikely that he would reveal that he had kidnapped me. I, who had been playing a major role in averting the kidnapping of the Prince and Princess, had not been able to prevent my own kidnapping! I soon exhausted my appreciation of the bleak humour of that contrast and collapsed into a mood of profound despondency.

I then remembered John Bunyan's wonderful book, *Pilgrim's Progress*, and his warning not to fall into the Slough of Despond. I must put my trust in the Lord, I admonished myself. And I concentrated.

Although Private Smith was a powerfully built man, I reckoned that he would not be taking me very far to his hiding place. I should contrive to drop something near that place, an item that would hint to the observant searcher that I was in the area. I would be moved in the dark, so there was every chance that my captor would not see it. The obvious object was a shoe. I slithered, bent my knees and tried to force my fingers to reach my feet to loosen one or other of the shoes. They would not reach. Something I could reach in the church? Not a very good idea. I could only move in a shuffle round the pillar. And, in any case, the building was abandoned. All that lingered was the smell of brandy. The derelict place was a perfect hideaway for smugglers (who seemed to know every inch of the Sussex coast) – ideal for depositing and collecting their contraband goods.

My head was still painful, too painful to allow me to relax; also, the ropes were chafing my wrists, especially after the effort of trying to remove a shoe. I then recalled the reason for my having taken my fateful walk. I had so enjoyed looking at the scenery during my ramble and had, not surprisingly, been so preoccupied since the attack, that I had not given my mind over to the quiet contemplation I had promised myself. In the silent, darkening environment where I then lay, I had no excuse.

I at first thought that there were three topics to ponder on: the kidnap plot, the murder, and my relationship with Mary. I quickly concluded, however, that there was no point in trying to think any more about the kidnapping: everything that could be considered already had been, and even if I were rescued in time to play my appointed role in Marlborough House, that too was settled. Bringing Jonathan's murderer to justice did worry me, though. Surely I could think of something to make that more certain. Ned North was the obvious suspect, as I and my friends all kept saying, yet neither we nor the constable had been able to find absolutely firm evidence. Mr North was bound to be picked up at the time of the attempted abduction, and then his cottage and his person could be thoroughly searched for the watch.

On the other hand, as my quiet and careful contemplation then made me realise, I had been having nagging doubts. Supposing the murderer was one of the other conspirators? Supposing the murder had no connection with the plot? That was the worst of all possibilities – we could have no notion of the attacker's motive and consequently no possibility of even guessing at his identity. Might the watch be the only clue if this was the case? I kept coming back to the watch. Who was wearing it at the churchyard? Was that fleeting observer of the funeral Ned North? Or someone completely different, though almost certainly a resident of Brighthelmston, for how else to explain his presence at St Nicholas Church? I decided that I should speak again to Jane. When I first questioned her, she was suffering from the shock of her fiancé's death. Perhaps, after the lapse of time, she would be able to talk in more detail, to remember little items of conversation that might throw some light on the assault.

The same was true of Mary, of course. But there was another subject I knew I must broach with her – that I should ask her if she would marry me sometime in the future. Both she and her father might think it an impertinent question because I had no imminent prospect of earning an income large enough to sustain a household of two – or more. Even so, a proposal of marriage seemed right. It would have two advantages. One was that, if Mary agreed, it would spur me on to seek preferment in the church, my own parish, perhaps, or a cathedral appointment. I would need a lot of help – my friend Tom and my vicar Thomas had connections. The other advantage would be for Mary. I knew in my heart that she loved me as much as I loved her. She would not be looking for anyone else as a husband. I owed it to her to make my intentions clear.

I was almost feeling grateful that Silas Smith had – temporarily, I hoped – incapacitated me physically so that I could concentrate on mental activity!

He returned at nightfall, as he had promised (or threatened). He placed a hunk of bread and a pitcher of water before me, removed the gag from my mouth and took his mallet from his belt – no doubt to deter me from shouting. He bade me eat and drink, awkward operations with my wrists bound. He then retied my gag.

After this grateful, albeit short-lived, interlude, Private Smith apologised for causing me discomfort, assuring me that it was essential, the while untying the rope round the pillar. As he was concentrating on these activities, I, taking advantage of the darkness, made another, desperate effort to loosen my left shoe: I had remembered that my left foot was very slightly shorter than my right. Pushing with all my strength with my right heel on the heel of my left shoe, I succeeded in easing it down an inch.

My kidnapper hefted me on to his shoulder and carried me out of the church. A weakly glowing moon struggled to cast a little light through the cloud. We covered, I assessed, about a hundred yards. He then lay me on the ground. We were at an army cart. I pressed my right shoe-heel again to the top of the left. The private folded back the tarpaulin that covered the wagon. My left shoe, with agonising reluctance, slowly shifted and dropped to the ground. Silas Smith picked me up, decanted me into the vehicle, climbed in and tied my wrists to a metal lashing ring in the end of the cart. Having jumped out, he spread the tarpaulin back as my roof. This was my prison. I felt certain that the chances of anyone finding me were minimal. And yet, as I heard the soldier quickly walk off, I reasoned that he had not noticed my discarded shoe: he had certainly not – my worst fear – tripped over it.

Despite my discomfort and mounting despair obscuring my earlier comfort from Mr Bunyan, I did, in fact, manage to doze fitfully.

In the depth of night, as I judged, I woke, hearing slight noises. Perhaps the noises had, in fact, broken my slumber. I listened intently. There were some slight cracks in the timbers of the wagon. I moved as well as I could. Luckily my captor had tied my hands to the ring with a cord of some length. I shuffled so as to place an eye to one of these slits in order to peer in the direction from which the sounds were coming. By that time, the moon was totally blanketed in thick cloud. However, I could just see the flickering of a lantern by the church door and dimly make out some movements. Smugglers were taking casks, barrels and boxes into the abandoned building. If only I could have shouted. I did, nevertheless, kick frantically with my one shoe against the wall of the cart. The effect was the dowsing of the light! The smugglers, it was clear, had heard my buffeting and did not wish to be seen by whoever was making the sound. They doubtless completed their clandestine business and crept away, dashing my hopes.

At dawn I became aware of daylight seeping into the cart through the chinks and under the edges of the tarpaulin. Then, eventually, distant voices; joyously, the faint but unmistakable sounds of James and Mary calling my name. With unbelievable good fortune, their voices grew louder as they neared my prison. I summoned all my breath to call through the thick cloth covering my mouth. It was a puny sound. I kicked hard as loud a tattoo as I could on the wooden wall. The volume was still not great enough, for the sounds of their voices shouting

'Ben' started to recede. It was utterly impossible for me then to stop my rapid plunge into the Slough of Despond. I prayed and prayed, fighting back sobs of despair.

Even so, God forgave me. For, immediately, I heard the bark of a dog coming in my direction. It transpired that he was my liberator.

After all these intervening years, dear reader, I have difficulty in recalling without choking emotion what then happened. The master of this hound was a Hove villager named Ebenezer Elliott. When he rose, somewhat late, that Sunday morning and left his cottage to feed his three pigs, he discovered that one of these precious animals was missing. He summoned his collie, Dan, to go in search of the errant sow. In due course their attempts to locate her brought them close to the church. Whereupon, Dan's nose scented at some distance my discarded shoe. Naturally, he would not mistake footwear for swine, but there was still human warmth and smell there. The object just had to be investigated and his master just had to be told. I looked out through my cracks and witnessed this unbelievable scene.

Dan barked; Ebenezer shouted to return him to his task of tracking down the pig; I kicked frenziedly; Dan barked loudly and frantically. Consequently, Ebenezer had no choice but to discover the reason for his dog's behaviour. I saw him drawing near. I kicked rhythmically to indicate that the source of the knocking was human. I heard him say to Dan, 'How did this shoe get here?' Then, hearing at last through the noise his dog was making, he said, 'and who d'ye think is making that knocking sound, eh?'

In an instant, the tarpaulin was flung back and I saw the rubicund face of my human rescuer. He hauled me out of the wagon, untied my gag and cords and massaged my sore wrists and ankles. He then carefully assisted me in my hobbling gait to the church, where he helped me sit down in a dusty pew. For my part, I just let forth a great outpouring of gratitude. Dan barked his pride at being proved right and licked my hands in friendship.

Then, through the open door, I heard my name called.

'Are you Ben?' Ebenezer asked.

'Yes,' I said, 'and they are my friends come to find me.' For the voices were those of Mary and James!

They came into the church, James guiding a pig by means of a stick!

I started to introduce James and Mary when Ebenezer and James embraced each other. They had, as I should have worked out myself, known each other very well so many years before when James had lived and worked in Hove. And so James introduced Mary, whom Ebenezer was evidently delighted to meet. Naturally, Ebenezer, James and Mary wanted to know what had happened to me. Ebenezer and I wanted to know how James had come to be in attendance with Ebenezer's nomadic pig.

I explained to James and Mary how Dan and Mr Elliott had found me bound and gagged in the army wagon and the clue I had dropped in the form of my shoe. I did not mention that James and Mary had not been quite near enough a little earlier to hear my knocking – they would have felt, quite erroneously, of course, so incompetent in the searching.

More difficult was explaining how I had come to be in that predicament. I could not possibly mention Private Smith to Ebenezer. I told a lie, and worried at the facility with which I was now making plausible falsehoods. I told the basic story reasonably accurately, but, instead of the soldier as the designer of my captivity, I substituted smugglers checking the inside of the church in preparation for their later, night-time operation. Mr Elliott found my tale perfectly credible, and that was what was important. I was not sure at the time about the reaction of James and Mary. They told me later that they thought that what had happened to me might have been connected with our investigations.

I was impatient to ask how James and Mary had come to be at the church and how they had found the pig.

James explained what had happened. Mrs Heath met

Thomas on his way to the church. He was convinced that something untoward had occurred, so truncated his sermon, hurried the celebrants through the communion, apologising to the congregation. He ran back to the vicarage, saddled up his speediest horse and rode at full gallop to the Preston's home. They were still at church. Accordingly, he frantically rode to St Nicholas church and, signalling to Tom Hudson, drew James and Mary out of the congregation.

They, of course, had no real idea where I might be, though Mary suggested that, because of my interest in church architecture, I could well have taken my walk to see the ruined Hove building. The alternatives, to Lewes or to Newhaven or roaming aimlessly, she thought less likely because of the longer distances involved. All three assumed that I had somewhere fallen down a steep slope in a deserted spot and, because of an injury, was unable to walk. They devised the following plan: James and Mary would take a curving walk across the Downs to Hove, looking about and calling my name, while Thomas would return to Rottingdean, ask Thomas Beard to ride across the hills to Lewes, while he himself took the Newhaven direction in search of me or anyone who might have seen me.

James then explained about the pig: 'We failed to find you here, but as we were walking further, we found Mr Elliott's sow. I knew from my farming background that it must have wandered and become lost. I was wondering what to do – feeling now responsible for two lost bodies! – when I heard Dan's barking and Mr Elliott's loud admonishments that they were looking for a pig. Therefore, I found a tree and broke a branch from it. I used this first to scratch the pig's back and thus gain its trust and then to guide it towards the voices, which, I felt, the pig had recognised, in any case. You can imagine how Mary and I were overwhelmed to find you here, Ben.'

It was a fairy-tale: villager, dog, pig, bookshop owner, his daughter and I were all as happy as we could be. Except that walking was somewhat uncomfortable for me. Ebenezer –

we had agreed to use Christian names – suggested that James and he help me to his cottage to refresh myself bodily by taking some food and drink and further massaging my wrists and ankles. I gladly agreed, and all five of us made our way from the church. Once we were installed in the cottage – the pig, of course, in its sty – James asked if Ebenezer had a cart we could use to convey me back to Rottingdean. The villager said he had one that would accommodate us all – that is, Ebenezer, Dan, James, Mary and me – though a little mucky, but he could provide sacks for us to sit upon.

It therefore happened that, when I was sufficiently restored, we made our way eastwards. As we passed the church and the edge of the campsite I noticed Silas Smith walking towards the wagon with bread and water. No one else in our party saw him. I, however, peering over the rim of Ebenezer's cart and thus unlikely to be seen by the soldier, enjoyed the sight of the private, as he lifted the tarpaulin, perplexed, angry and worried.

Our arrangement was that Ebenezer should first stop at Brighthelmston, to allow James and Mary to return home, and then take me on to Rottingdean. During that first portion of the journey, James and Ebenezer talked about their old times in Hove and about their separate and different lives since. Mary and I talked about my captivity, I giving brief, discrete, indeed secretive, indications of the true identity of my captor without Ebenezer hearing or understanding; this was so very tantalising for us both. Even more tantalising was the fact that I had to leave her in order to be taken home by Ebenezer. During that stretch of the journey we inevitably talked about my friendship with James and Mary, and Jonathan's murder, though, again, I thought it wise not to mention my connection with that dreadful event.

Having arrived at Mrs Heath's cottage, I thanked Ebenezer yet again and promised to visit him in friendship in the near future. Mrs Heath was overwhelming in her emotional welcome, tears flooding down her old handsome cheeks. I declined her insistent offer of food, explaining that the man who had just dropped me at her door had recently seen to my needs. I then had to give her the version of my tale that I had told Ebenezer, ensuring that my voice could be heard above Bill's purring as he demonstrated his pleasure at my return. She sat open-mouthed, interjecting at frequent intervals, 'you poor thing', 'you poor man', 'how awful'. When I had at last finished my story, I told her that I had to be away again the following night and that I would explain the complicated reason when I returned, insisting that I should repeat my story to Dr Hooker without delay. She fully understood.

Thomas was agog during my narration. At its conclusion he congratulated me on my courage, inventiveness and good fortune. I felt awkward; I was deeply conscious of my frailty during the ordeal, my periods of profound despondency and pessimism. I confessed these moods to my vicar. He comforted me by saying that not everyone is endowed with the self-control of a saint and that I had assuredly learned a great deal about myself from this ordeal.

Thomas explained the efforts that he and Mr Beard had made to find me. I therefore went to the latter's house to thank him and to explain my capture and rescue. And then, at last, home, to sleep. I needed to be in good fettle the next day: it was Monday, 17th June.

After a hearty breakfast, and armed with my sword-stick, I set forth to Brighthelmston. Although my weapon would have been useless against Silas Smith's stealthy and sudden bludgeoning from behind, I thought it sensible to carry it that morning. He knew that I had escaped, and might try another, this time, mortal attack. He must have been feeling very worried, not just because of the threat I now posed to him, but also because the black clouds were heavy with rain as far as the eye could see. Even though, as James had told me, the army commanders and townspeople had agreed to his suggested fireworks display, the likelihood of its taking place was remote.

I spent most of the morning with James and Mary. I thanked them again for the efforts they had made to find me and narrated my adventure in complete detail, including the purpose of my walk to the remains of St Andrew's Church. I returned to that at the end of my tale, to the thoughts that I had turned over in my mind while in captivity. First, I shared with them my unease about ensuring the arrest and conviction of Jonathan's murderer. Mary said that she had often tried to remember anything that might help, but without success, but suggested that I might take the opportunity to broach the subject with Jane at Marlborough House that evening while awaiting the abductors' arrival. I thanked her for that idea.

Then I stuttered into my other topic I needed to express to Mary and her father. Although I had been rehearsing what I should say while Betsy conveyed me at her sedate pace from Rottingdean, I was still tongue-tied. I managed to utter in a great stammering rush my proposal of marriage with all the problems and hesitations attending my status and financial condition. Happily, the looks on their faces encouraged me. James grasped my hand, and said how delighted he was. Neither of us could possibly have doubted for a second Mary's feelings that were displayed so frankly on her face.

'Kiss the joyous girl,' James instructed. No hesitation inhibited me then!

James scuttled around, collecting a bottle of wine and three glasses so that he could toast Mary and me as the blissful couple, and that we could join the vinous celebration.

I could scarcely believe my good fortune. James made some lame excuse to go out, so that Mary and I could be alone. We held hands and kissed more passionately than the decorous embrace we engaged in during her father's presence. We chattered effervescently, about what neither of us could accurately remember even the next day.

At length James returned. I said that, though it grieved me to leave them, I should go back to Rottingdean to tell Thomas and Mrs Heath my wonderful news, and also to prepare myself for the climax of these eventful weeks – at Marlborough House, that evening or night, we knew not exactly when.

Reminded of the planned ambush of the kidnappers and my involvement in the ambuscade, Mary bit her lip in anxiety and fear. We could not be truly happy until this dreadful business was concluded.

Chapter 14

Nothing could go wrong, surely. I kept thinking this as I rode to Marlborough House. Was Betsy bored with these constant journeys to Brighthelmston, or did she enjoy the walks? 'That's right,' I said to myself, 'stop worrying and turn your mind to something else.' But I couldn't. I even tried to wonder if Betsy disliked the rain. There was no point in speculating, because she must have been inured to it. In any case, the rain had stopped. This observation led me to realise that the firework display would take place. My thoughts were back to concerns for the coming evening and night, forgetting Betsy.

We arrived at about seven o'clock. One of Mr Hamilton's servants took care of Betsy; the morose manservant, Henry, whose surname for some reason I did not know, led me into the house, relieved me of my outer clothing (though I naturally kept my sword-stick with me) and then accompanied me to a room where the Prince's civilian guests were to assemble.

The Prince, the Princess and Mr Hamilton welcomed me in turn. Out of courtesy, I took the proffered glass of wine, but explained that I would partake of this refreshment meagrely because I was concerned that my reactions should not be clouded or retarded at the critical moment. The Prince laughed, though said seriously, 'Good for you, Reverend Sydenham.'

He then asked me what I had been doing since we last met. I was reluctant to relate my story in full for fear of becoming a boring centre of attention and excluding others from the conversation. However, as it became evident that I was summarising my recent eventful days, the Prince constantly interrupted, demanding to be told all the details.

When I stopped at my deliverance from the army wagon, the Prince said, 'Mr Sydenham, I envy you the excitement you have recently enjoyed; a mere prince could never hope to equal it.' Had he, I wondered, entirely pushed from his mind any thought that he might be taken that night by force to France? Indeed, he immediately smiled and looked round for approbation of his witticism. The desired reaction was led by Princess Caroline.

'Do not misunderstand me, sir,' he continued. 'You have acted and suffered with exemplary courage on behalf of myself and Her Royal Highness. When we first met and laid our plans at Windsor, I did not conceive for a second that you would be personally exposed to such perils as you have experienced. I most humbly thank you and beg your forgiveness.'

Mr Wickham soon arrived and, after a few pleasantries, he asked that everyone in the house should be assembled in the large octagonal dining room. Servants and soldiers were summoned.

He then addressed us all. 'I want us all to be clear, as far as we can be,' he said, 'what will happen tonight. 'You servants and soldiers have been told only that Their Royal Highnesses wish to feel safe while they are staying in this house; Mr Hamilton is in frail health and there are few robust men servants in residence; hence our visiting infantrymen. It was imperative that we kept absolutely secret the presence of these soldiers and the detailed reasons for their being here. I must now inform you of these.'

The government official then gave an account of the plot and our plan to foil it, though skimming over the believed major involvement of the French – the secret services need to preserve some of their secrets. But he did stress most forcibly that certainly the leaders of this outrageous plot should be apprehended alive so that they could be interrogated in case there be others 'behind the scenes', as he put, whom he would want to hunt down. He introduced me as the person in the room who would be most able to recognise the leaders we knew about. The inevitable reaction of those who had been kept in ignorance of the plot, as you, dear reader, can imagine, was one of horror, and they exchanged agitated comments among themselves expressing this emotion.

'I come now to the arrangements for the coming hours,' he said. 'My agents are already in place to apprehend any of the would-be kidnappers who escape from here. For those of you who do not already know, the military and civil authorities have agreed to a fireworks display. It was suggested by one of the conspirators as a distraction: the crowds and noise at the entertainment would assist the entry of the abductors undetected into this house. To have denied authorisation might have aroused suspicion among this band and even an aborting of the scheme. Our plan to arrest some of the kidnappers might then have failed. The entertainment is due to take place from 10 to 11 o'clock, in The Steyne. The Prince and Princess are to watch it from the upper windows of this house, illuminated so that the crowds can cheer Their Royal Highnesses and witness their enjoyment of this expression of loyalty. The front door will be in darkness and in so far as people will be looking in this direction, rather than at the fireworks, they will be focusing on the windows of the top storey. The abductors should thus be able to gain fairly easy access, though, of course, we do not know which doors or windows they will use.'

I found all this information useful, as I had not learned about these details before.

Mr Wickham continued: 'It seems to me that the conspirators have two optional plans, for which they consider the fireworks display would give them an advantage. We need to be aware of these in devising our counter-measures.

'One, is for them to enter before the display starts and before people gather for it, when The Steyne would be empty. They would plan to shut everyone in a back room – and,

157

remember, they have no idea that there are bodyguards in the house. Then they would strip the Prince of his jacket and necktie and the Princess of her dress and both of their wigs, fit them with less expensive wear, and two of their number would don these royal clothes to appear at the windows pretending to be Their Royal Highnesses. In the dim light that would be available, the ruse could work. Then, after the display, as the crowd is dispersing, the Prince and Princess, bound and gagged, would be bundled into a carriage without undue notice. If that is their plan, we must expect our "guests" to arrive, say, at about nine o'clock.

'The alternative would be for them to force their entry at about a quarter-to-eleven, by which time the Prince and Princess could well be expected to have withdrawn from the window and they could be bundled into a conveyance after the crowds had gone home soon after. In this case, we should be particularly alert at about half-past-ten.'

Mr Hamilton said, 'Might they not be most likely to come in the dead of night when the town is asleep?'

'That is a possibility, true,' Mr Wickham politely acknowledged, 'but then why go to the trouble of asking for a firework display to use as a diversion from their activities?'

We all agreed that we should be at our places in the house from about nine o'clock. Mr Wickham ended his address by repeating to the soldiers that we wished to take the leaders alive. He dismissed the servants and took the soldiers to their positions, instructing them on the particular importance of each in relation to observing the ground outside, guarding the entrance hall and guarding the room where the Prince and Princess would stay until the start of the fireworks and music.

Nine o'clock came, and all was quiet. The Steyne was deserted and remained so until the crowds began to arrive about half-past the hour. The fireworks started to send forth their glorious and exciting effects, the band played with verve and the royal couple took up their positions to watch them and acknowledge the crowd. The display ended, and still there had been no intrusion. Had Mr Hamilton's suggestion been right? We waited tensely... hour after hour. Nothing happened. We asked each other, why not? We had been so certain that the attempt at abduction was going to take place and that the evening or night of 17th June was the planned date.

Soon after dawn, the Prince came to see Mr Wickham (he and I were stationed together) and suggested that the danger had passed. 'A damp squib, eh?' he said, and we relieved our tension with appreciative laughter. They agreed that the servants should provide everyone with breakfast, that afterwards the soldiers should be sent back to their barracks and I should go home. Mr Wickham would dismiss his agents on the beach and ask if they had any explanation for the abduction attempt having been abandoned. He would then return to Marlborough House to sleep for a while before returning to London.

When I left I went straight to see Mary and James to show them that I was uninjured and to report the puzzle of the uneventful evening and night. They, it goes without saying, were both relieved and perplexed. I took my leave fairly quickly, not just to catch up with my sleep, but to discover what, if anything, had happened in Rottingdean. I promised to let them know later that day.

Dr Hooker was sure to have all the information about the smugglers' landing in the village, and, of course, he would be on tenterhooks to hear about the happenings in Brighthelmston. Consequently, I indicated to Betsy that I wished to go direct to the vicarage.

Thomas was glad to discover that I was unaffected by my hours in Marlborough House, apart from my bleary eyes, and was astonished at my news.

'Something must have gone awry with that main part of the plot because the landing we expected here did take place. The smugglers were overwhelmed by the collective weight the preventive forces had mobilised. They were furious at being duped, because – and we had expected this, of course –

the barrels and boxes contained no contraband items at all, just innocently legal goods such as fish, salt beef, boots and clothing! A few of the smugglers played the game of escaping through our subterranean tunnels; those arrested had to be released. The conspirators' ruse had succeeded.'

'But what about Will Watson?' I asked with some concern.

'Ah, he was the exception,' said Thomas. 'Your friend, Mr Nepean turned up. He spoke to the commander of our Customs House, who told me the whole story last night. Mr Nepean formally identified Will and ordered that he be arrested. He justified this demand by referring to the conversation that, he was sure, one or more of the customs men, if not the commander himself, must have heard and therefore could corroborate. Poor Will was brought forward. He was aghast, almost collapsed, in fact.'

'Since the attack on Marlborough House did not in fact take place, he cannot be accused of a specially serious crime,' I said. 'Even so, we must do everything possible to help his family. I will see to that.'

'I thought you would,' Thomas replied.

I went home. I apologised to Mrs Heath for not telling her immediately the reason for my overnight absence because I urgently needed to sleep first. I have never been able to cope with a short ration of sleep. This was almost the worst aspect of my adventures at that time.

I had barely been awake after that needed rest but was already dressed when I heard a heavy knocking on the cottage door. Mrs Heath opened it. Outside was a messenger – obviously for me. He asked me to confirm my identity and I invited him in to my room. I thought I recognised him. When he spoke it was clear to me where I had seen him.

He said, 'I am in the service of His Royal Highness, the Prince of Wales, and bear a message from him. He is arranging a dinner at Marlborough House this evening to celebrate the failure of the plot to kidnap him and Her Royal Highness, Princess Caroline. The guests will be those whom he wishes

160

to thank for their noble involvement in this affair. His Royal Highness would be most honoured by your presence.'

I responded: 'Please tell His Royal Highness that it is I who am honoured by this most gracious invitation and look forward with the utmost pleasure to being at Marlborough House this evening.'

'Thank you,' said the messenger. 'The Prince will expect you at eight o'clock.'

He then left. I calculated that I should leave some time between six and seven o'clock, so that my route to Marlborough House could take me via the home of my fiancée in order to be able to tell her and James about the events in Rottingdean and my invitation to dine again with the Prince.

I then asked Mrs Heath to sit with me while I ate my belated breakfast so that I could honour my promise of explaining my absence the previous night and the consequent visit of the messenger. As the Rottingdean landing had been handled to our satisfaction and the kidnapping had evidently been aborted, I felt that there was no danger in revealing the outline of the crisis, which, naturally, I had kept secret.

She was greatly distressed at hearing about the plot. 'He's a ne'er-do-well, that's for sure,' she said, 'but he's the heir to the throne, and I wouldn't wish him to come to no harm, nor his new wife.'

I sneezed, and went to my room to fetch a handkerchief. I sneezed again.

'Now you've gone and caught yourself a cold,' she said. 'It's this nasty weather, and you being out all hours. When you go out this evening, you be sure to wrap yourself up properly. I'll see that you do.'

True to her word, Mrs Heath fussed about my clothes, making sure that I was wearing my best shoes and that I had a clean handkerchief. *I* made sure that I took my sword-stick: Private Smith was still at large, though I planned that, on the following day, I would go to the camp to report his attack on me to the colonel and have the man arrested.

The journey was uneventful, the weather, clement. James opened the door. He looked somewhat different. The immediate thought that came to my mind was that he looked as he did at the funeral. It took me a few seconds to work out the explanation – an embarrassing moment of silence. The reason for this unusual appearance was that he had brushed and combed his usually unkempt hair and was wearing his best suit. Then, quick as a flash, I realised: James and Mary had received an invitation too! So Mary and I could celebrate our engagement with a royal dinner!

Mary took a little time to join us – she had not expected me. She looked splendid in her birthday-present dress. We were all very happy. I gave them the news about the previous night's happenings in Rottingdean, then more about the evening and night on guard in Marlborough House. When we left to walk to The Steyne, I made sure I was carrying my newly acquired weapon, explaining to James and Mary my worry about Private Smith.

When we arrived at Marlborough House, we were ushered in by the manservant, whom Mary knew because of her visits to Jane. 'Good evening, Mr Hook,' she said to him. So that was Henry's surname.

We left our coats and hats and my sword-stick in a closet and were led to the Drawing Room. The Prince graciously welcomed Mary and said how pleased he was to see her again. I introduced Mary and James to the Princess and to the other guests whom they had not previously met. It transpired that there were just five other guests: Mr Nepean, Mr Wickham (who, because of the dinner, had delayed his return to London), the commanding officers of the camp and infantry barracks and – a lovely touch – the Prince's friend and the source of our intelligence about the plot, Martha Gunn. Therefore, with Mr Hamilton, we made a total of ten.

I quickly reported to the camp colonel that Private Smith had assaulted me, but we agreed that the occasion was not right to enter into details; that would have spoiled the party atmosphere. Somehow or other, in the pre-prandial chattering, Martha discovered that Mary and I had just become affianced.

To our intense embarrassment, she shouted out, 'Your Royal Highnesses, ladies and gentlemen, I have an important announcement to make.' And told them our personal news. There were calls of 'congratulations!' and 'hope you will both be happy' in the bass register and Mrs Gunn's deep alto, overtopped by the uncontrolled shriek of 'wonderful!' uttered by Jane Patcham, who was in attendance to look after her employer.

As she came over to congratulate us I recalled that I had forgotten to ask her the previous day if she could think again about who might have been Jonathan's murderer: most unfortunate, because I would have no opportunity to talk to her in private during the dinner. I determined to return the following day to have that conversation.

The repast was a banquet, even outdoing the dinner I had enjoyed a fortnight before. To ease the digestion of such quantities of food and because eating was in any case interrupted by so much talking, the meal progressed at a slow pace.

At nearly eleven o'clock I sneezed. I had totally forgotten about my cold. Worse than that single sneeze, I soon sneezed and coughed several times. I searched for my handkerchief. Without success: I realised that I must have put it in my coat pocket. I was in desperate need of it, so I had no alternative but to excuse myself from the table in order to go to the closet to fetch it. I was overcome with shame.

I had just entered the closet when there was a knock on the front door. One of the men servants went to open it.

I heard him grunt as he was knocked to the floor by a hard blow. There followed the barely audible sound of stealthy footsteps. I grabbed my handkerchief and pressed it to my nose, willing myself with all the concentration I could command not to sneeze and reveal my presence, then, silently, took hold of my sword-stick.

I peered gingerly into the Hall: the servant lay unconscious. By this time, the intruders had penetrated into the house. There were three of them and they were making for the dining room, from whence sounds of talking could easily be heard. They hesitated, turned to whisper to each other, enough for me to recognise them: Ned North, Silas Smith and Louis Lemâitre. Luckily, they were completely unaware of me, for, their intent was obvious. Although the full-scale operation to kidnap the Prince and Princess had, for some reason, been called off on the appointed day, these three were determined to abduct them now.

They walked boldly into the room. I crept cautiously after them, hugging the wall. As the diners saw the conspirators, they fell utterly silent.

M. Lemâitre, acting as their spokesman, said, 'Your Royal Highnesses, we have come to take you to another place. For the rest of you, remain in your chairs and put your hands on the table while we arrange for the Prince and Princess to accompany us. We wish harm neither to them nor to any of you, but we are well armed and will not hesitate to use our weapons if any attempt is made to prevent us from accomplishing our mission.'

Not all the servants were in the dining room, so I hastened down the corridor to the kitchen, where I found three cooks and Henry. I quietly explained what was happening and asked them to arm themselves with suitable utensils to employ as missiles or weapons and the sharpest pointed knives.

Henry insisted on entering the dining room from the kitchen, so that he would be facing the kidnappers. I and the cooks went down the corridor so as to enter the dining room behind them. Just as we made our appearance, Mr Hamilton rose from his chair, tried to say something but collapsed with a seizure. Jane, whose job it was to look after the ailing politician and was standing near him, moved to his aid.

Ned North yelled, 'Stay where you are!' and levelled his pistol at Jane. In an instant, Henry flung himself in front of

Jane to protect her. The coastguard discharged his pistol. The manservant slumped down.

Chaos ensued. A heavily-built cook felled M. Lemâitre with a hefty blow on the head with a weighty copper saucepan; another cook grabbed Mr North and thrust the point of his knife at the villain's throat to prevent him from moving; and, as Private Smith drew a pistol from his belt, I lunged with the blade of my sword-stick, piercing his hand so that the gun dropped harmlessly un-cocked to the floor. James leapt up to seize the pistol and make sure that its owner did not make his escape. Meanwhile Messrs Wickham and Nepean hustled the Prince and Princess away from the turmoil into the kitchen.

I then rushed to the manservant's assistance. He looked severely wounded, blood pouring from a wound in his chest. My immediate thought was: Ned North's second victim; what a hideous person he must be. And, as with the dying Jonathan, so this man desperately wanted to tell me something.

His voice was the faintest whisper. He said, 'I killed Jonathan Preston. I was mad with jealousy. I love Jane.'

Mary was now by me and heard the confession. She said, 'When the pistol-ball struck him I heard a ringing sound.'

I put my hand in the dying man's inside breast pocket and pulled out a watch with blood and an indentation on its edge. The ball from Ned North's pistol had struck the watch before ricocheting and penetrating Henry Hook's chest. This impact had activated the chiming mechanism in the watch, Jonathan's watch with the portrait of the fair Jane Patcham.

Chapter 15

Jonathan's murder was resolved, his killer had met a just fate, and the Prince and Princess had been saved from being kidnapped. In a sense, therefore, my story is ended. Yet, after that night of Tuesday, 18th June 1795 there were loose ends to be tied into the tale and consequent events to be reported. So, here, in the way of an epilogue are a few more pages to bring my account to a tidy conclusion.

You are, I am sure, dear reader, curious to know why the plan to abduct Their Royal Highnesses did not come to pass in its originally designed manner. I must therefore set down the explanation for this first of all. The following week Mr Nepean sent a messenger to inform me out of courtesy the reason for this mystery.

The conspirators had been confounded by a relatively minor episode in Britain's conduct of the war with France. This was the *émigré* expedition, to the tiny Quiberon peninsula jutting out from the southern coast of Brittany, organised with the objective of assisting the people there fighting against the Republican government. In fact, before the event Mr Nepean had briefly and confidentially told me about this force setting forth on 17th June. When he mentioned the operation I was struck by the coincidence of the date of the sailing of that little army and the planned kidnapping, as I have already recorded. I thought that, somehow, the conspirators would be helped, and that they knew they would be helped, by the concentration of our naval power, progressing in the opposite direction, away from Brighthelmston, that is, from Southampton to Quiberon. What the messenger had to report to me was the very converse.

It happened thus. Not only did our navy provide an escort for the *émigré* army, it was also considered circumspect to supplement this protection by ensuring that no French warships were at sea in the Channel at all. Therefore, while Commodore Borlase Warren commanded a modest squadron to convoy the vessels conveying the soldiers, Admiral Lord Bridport took the Channel Fleet on a thorough sweep to engage any French ships that might be a menace.

Apparently, the French boat, that was to sail to Brighthelmston and be met on the evening of 17th June by the three conspirators we knew about, set forth just as Lord Bridport's formidable fleet was passing the Normandy coast. Presumably, though we shall never know for certain, by the time the French kidnappers judged it safe to cross the Channel, they were afraid that Messrs North, Smith and Lemâitre (Watson being engaged in Rottingdean) would no longer be waiting for them because these three might attract suspicion for lingering on the beach for so long. No one without sinister intent would spend extended time there in the unpleasant low temperature.

As it turned out, the Quiberon landing was a dreadful fiasco. One of the many casualties was the Chevalier de Saint-Paul: a pointless waste of the life of a fine man. Even so, unbeknown to the French and British commanders involved, the launching of the expedition gave a strange, albeit fortuitous, twist to the main strand of my tale.

Mr Nepean's messenger also informed me that, after 'the Battle of Marlborough House' the three English conspirators had been rapidly taken to Lewes jail and interrogated in an attempt to glean information about the French devisers of the plot – to no avail, because they were doubtless kept in ignorance about the scale and significance of the operation. Even so, the government authorities harboured no doubts that the Committee of Public Safety in Paris were the originators of the plot. The three English traitors were executed by firing squad. There was no public trial. The incident was so sensitive that everything possible was done to keep all aspects completely secret. No newspapers at the time or subsequent books about that period of history or about the Prince have contained any mention of the plot. This, my account, is the only record.

As to Louis Lefebvre/Lemaître, shame to tell, he managed to escape from Marlborough House in the confusion. The blow on the head with the saucepan had stunned him only momentarily and when James's attention was distracted by Henry Hook's confession that he had killed his son, the Frenchman must have crawled away.

As to the Prince and Princess of Wales, sad to say, their relationship soured, even to the scandalous extent that, when the Prince succeeded his father, as George IV, he had Queen Caroline banned from the coronation ceremony in Westminster Abbey; what one would have thought was an unbelievable event in the history of our royal family.

Yet the man who treated his wife in this awful manner, and the central figure in our tale, as, successively, Prince of Wales, Prince Regent and King, retained a keen affection for Brighton (as I must now, with some reluctance, call the town). Because of his father's severe disability, the Prince of Wales became the Prince Regent in 1811. This new status, he considered, warranted a personal palace of some splendour. Consequently, by a number of accretions, the modest Marine Pavilion was transformed into a building of exquisite or vulgar design, depending on one's taste, of overt oriental style. As Prince Regent he loved Brighton and his Pavilion; as King, less so. He died in 1830, a few years before my writing of this manuscript.

I cannot, in truth, say that I thought him to be a fitting person to be our country's monarch. And yet, I do owe him a most signal debt of gratitude.

On 17th August, exactly two months after the French-planned kidnapping, I received a letter from the Prince of Wales.

It bore exciting news. In addition to renewed thanks for the part I had played in protecting Their Royal Highnesses, it contained information about a tangible and wonderful expression of his gratitude. He had approached the most notable landowners in Sussex who had church livings in their gift to ask them to ensure that, when a vacancy occurred, it should be offered to me. This had now happened, and within a few days I would be contacted about becoming the vicar of a parish in the north-east of the county.

Consequently, and not without considerable sadness, I left Rottingdean, making most heartfelt promises to visit my friends there often. Additional, really bitter causes for sadness at the time, was that Billy died six weeks before I left Mrs Heath's cottage and that Betsy, pining perhaps for her little companion, mortally declined in health soon after my removal to my new home. As consolation, they were both quite aged, and Billy chose to depart this world very sensibly: he would not have been happy to move to a new, strange home.

But the joyful implications of my preferment far outweighed the melancholy. My new stipend was quite generous, therefore I was able, once settled, to suggest to Mary without any qualms that we arrange a date for our wedding. This took place on Tuesday, 23rd September. The service was conducted by Thomas Hooker at St Margaret's Church, Tom Hudson was my best man and Jane Patcham was Mary's bridesmaid. Naturally, my parents and siblings attended the wedding. As a result, Jane met my brother Bernard and soon, they too married, their standard of living enhanced by a generous legacy left by Mr Hamilton to Jane in appreciation of her help in the last years of his life. He in fact died only eleven months after his seizure on the night of the attempted kidnapping – I have often wondered if that violence in his home hastened his death.

The day of my marriage to Mary was just under four months after I had found the man, who, had he lived, would have been my brother-in-law. And whose dying words I had so stupidly misconstrued. 'Mmm … gun' was not a hesitant 'gun', but

'Martha Gunn'. 'Private ... er ... meeting' was not 'private meeting', but a private soldier at a meeting with others. 'Prints' was not a reference to his etchings, but to the Prince. And, 'h-hook ... er', as I so belatedly discovered, was not a hesitant reference to Dr Hooker, but to Henry Hook.

How stupid I had been. This last clue was crucial; and it was obvious from the very beginning that Jonathan had no connection with Dr Hooker, yet I made no attempt to seek out an alternative explanation. Furthermore, this misunderstanding misled us all throughout those weeks of attempted detection. Henry Hook and Jane Patcham had worked together in Marlborough House. He became enamoured of this pretty girl, and, despite the fact that she gave him no encouragement in his advances, he was devastated when she became engaged to Jonathan.

I learned all this from Jane after that dreadful night when Mr Hook died defending her. Although she could never have forgiven him for killing her fiancé, she was inevitably shocked and gratified by his action in saving her. He had clearly stolen and kept the watch because it contained Jane's portrait, and it was obviously he who was lurking at Jonathan's funeral and whose watch the sexton heard chiming. Whether he intended to kill Jonathan or merely wound him we shall never know, though we may presume that the stealing of some of the prints, the importance of which I so misconstrued and exaggerated, was merely part of his attempt to simulate robbery as the motive for the attack.

If only I had got round to questioning Jane a second time, I might well have thought of Henry Hook as a suspect, instead of assuming so obstinately, despite my late, vague doubts, that the murderer was Ned North.

Not only was Mr North innocent of that crime, but my identification of him as the murderer also led us falsely to link the killing with the kidnapping plot.

I was guilty of the sin of arrogance in taking on the rôle of detective with the result that I inevitably displayed the incompetence of the untrained and inexperienced. I vowed never again to be distracted from my vocation as a priest. I had enough to learn about this work to keep me gainfully occupied. On the other hand, Mary has never agreed with my self-criticism. After all, without my plunging into those investigations, we would probably never have forged our deep friendship and been joined in holy matrimony.

Not only that – it had been exciting...

And I did break my vow...

Note

Although the story here narrated is fictional, the historical background is factual and faithfully recorded. To give a few examples: the exceptionally bad weather; the geographical features of the areas and architectural features of the buildings described; Dr Hooker's involvement in smuggling; the trial and punishment of the East Blatchington army mutineers; the establishment of the Aliens Office; the Quiberon expedition; the Prince of Wales being in residence at Windsor Castle at the time stated; the Prince of Wales's menu. There are two main exceptions. For dramatic purposes the visit of the Prince and Princess of Wales to stay at Marlborough House in June 1795 has been brought forward by ten days, starting on the 8th instead of the 18th of the month. Secondly, William Wickham did not absent himself from Berne to be in England at this time. Many of the characters are historical persons, as shown in the list at the beginning of the book and care has been taken to use only those words that were current in the late 18th century.

* * *

Acknowledgment

I am grateful to Mr Maurice Hutt,
formerly Reader in Modern French History
at the University of Sussex, for his friendle advice.

173